A Scientist's Remorse

A Scientist's Remorse

Ceara Comeau

ISBN 978-1-7335664-0-7 (Paperback Edition)
ISBN 978-1-7335664-1-4 (eBook Edition)

This novel's story is a work of fiction. Names, characters,
events and incidents are the products of the author's
imagination. Certain long-standing institutions, agencies,
and public offices are mentioned, but the characters
involved are wholly imaginary.

Edited by Stacey Longo
Cover Design by Stephen Lomer

Published in 2019 by Ceara Comeau

www.cearacomeau.com

❧◊❧

To the fans of

"Memories of Chronosalis"

This one's for you!

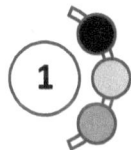

1

"Khyra, I promise, we'll leave in five minutes!"

Most children usually heard this statement from their parents when they grew bored with whatever activity their parents forced upon them. But I heard it every day.

"But Father, you said that forever ago!" I found myself saying far too often as a child . . . at which point, he would ignore my complaints and return to his conversation. I believe my mother pitied me, as she knew I hated the constant parties our family hosted and attended. My two older brothers and older sister reveled in his popularity. All they thought about was following in his footsteps. Not that they cared about his business endeavors; no, they wanted father's approval and money.

"Do you even know who Father is speaking to?" asked my eldest sibling, Richard, as the other two came to his side looking at me disapprovingly.

Just like my father, my siblings ignored my behavior during these gatherings. But this specific time was different, as if they were keeping a close watch on father's business dealings, expecting something great to take place at any moment. I shrugged my little shoulders and shook my head.

"Of course she wouldn't—Khyra is in her own world of daydreams. How would she recognize her own grandfather?" Bethany, the second oldest, snapped.

I glanced back at the man as he shook my father's hand. I recalled seeing him once or twice, although the purpose of our meeting was vague. He had tan skin and always wore an expensive-looking suit. His curly white hair was trimmed short. Not a hair stood out of place on his thin mustache. "Grandfather Lisbon," I remembered my siblings shouting every time he stepped through our door. He always brought fascinating gifts for the older children, but often forgot I existed. I didn't know if it was because I was different. I tried giving him the benefit of the doubt and attributed his forgetfulness to his old age, but I often wondered.

"Grandfather Lisbon will make us . . . I mean Father—rich!" exclaimed Daniel, who at this time was nine, five years older than me.

"Father already has money, right?" I asked, confused as to how wealth or fame worked.

Richard flashed a fake smile through gritted teeth as he knelt down to my level and tried to explain the situation. "If Grandfather Lisbon agrees to work with Father, then we'll have no need to worry about our future! We can carry on the family business Father has prepared for us!"

What kind of introduction was that? A rather solemn one. See, this conversation with my siblings was one of the few that I can recall. It was a point in my life where they actually seemed to want to help me understand what our life was about. There was no bickering—well, nothing verbal, that is. And it was a monumental turning point for me. It was at this very moment, I believe, that I finally understood what set me apart from my siblings. Even at four years old, I understood a few adult concepts, and the idea of carrying on where my rich father left off sounded boring.

I wasn't interested in building factories all over the world; I preferred to further my education aside from the typical private lessons I took as a child. Unlike my siblings, I took as many lessons as possible without my parents getting suspicious. My teachers loved my yearning for knowledge and even sneaked extra books into my homework assignments to satisfy my hungry brain. But that's not the only place where I received an education.

Albeit it was unconventional, but I met a friend while I was at a nearby playground. And it wasn't always easy escaping the confines of my home or ditching my father's security. Sometimes, while we were out and about, I'd slip behind them when they weren't looking or—my personal favorite—I'd claim I felt sick and stayed home from school. Our nannies, at this time, were too interested in their books or soap operas to care what I did. Now, what was so special about this friend that I'd go through all that? He liked me for who I was, and his family taught me more about life than my parents or teachers ever could. This friend was Emrys Bates.

He was of the Romani gypsy culture, and as such, was raised in a lifestyle filled with nomadic and naturalistic principles and a heavy belief of magic. He even showed me some of his tricks, most of which was predicting the future, something he had always done. Emrys never foresaw major events, but he did occasionally use his gift to gain the upper hand at games. It was funny at first, but eventually grew annoying. But his unusual and free lifestyle distracted me from the chaos at home. His parents seemed accepting of our friendship and would often help me come up with excuses as to why I was late for dinner.

And yet despite all the freedom and magic I witnessed through Emrys's perfect life, it couldn't distract me from the inevitable disaster mine contained. Every time I came home from one of our adventures, I learned of new developments in my father's career. Just as my siblings hoped, my father joined forces with Grandfather Lisbon and developed Crawlis Industries, a company with the sole desire for creating the perfect cleaning product. Well, perfect in *their* mindset, at least. They set up factories from Beijing all the way across the seas to the corner of the smallest town in Maine. My family became famous for our company's innovative products, and before I could even have time to fully comprehend the full extent of what was happening, the people in town didn't treat me as if I was my own person. Oh, no: they officially crowned me as Desmond's daughter, someone to be politely kept away at arm's length. With my family's fame progressing, I often sneaked out of the house late at night to see the family I wished I belonged to.

It was during these special times where Emrys's parents educated me on how factories like my father's affected the earth. Now, I didn't know much in respect to the Romani people as a whole and their way of life, but it seemed to me that the Bates family was very interested in protecting the environment. I suppose it had something to do with their magic; perhaps it didn't agree with the pollution that ignorant humans created. Either way, I never asked. I remember their warnings as if it were yesterday: fish mutations, filthy air, death to sea creatures, to say nothing of the poor seagulls who got caught in trash along the beaches. As a child, these facts made me scared and rather angry.

"There must be something we can do to stop them!" I exclaimed to Emrys's parents as they finished explaining what pollution was.

"I know, little one," Cornelius Bates encouraged. "Every one of us has a part to play in protecting our Mother Earth. But we cannot stop large factories like your father's. All we can do is lead by example."

"But you have magic, right? That must count for something!" I protested.

"Khyra, our magic is no match for your father. We can . . . we're limited to what our gifts allow us to do," said Emrys kindly. I knew there was more he wanted to say, but judging by the look Cornelius shot his way, I could tell he was stepping in dangerous territory.

As a child, I always understood far more than the adults in my life gave me credit for. This is not to say that I could comprehend everything going on, but I grasped the concept of what factories do. And in some cases, understood more than more than my sixteen-year-old brother did. I guess I was always different, but that was a part of my individuality that my family couldn't steal from me. Or so I thought. It was the end of this conversation that tore me away from Emrys forever. I had nearly finished my tea with Emrys and his family when a familiar voice rang out behind me.

"So, *this* is where you've been running off to. Your father and mother have been worried sick!"

I turned my head so fast I swear I heard a crack in my neck. John Oak, my cousin on my father's side, stood tall and proud. He was seven years older than me, and everyone in my family knew him as the snitch. Even my siblings detested him! My parents often used John's investigatory prowess to spy on us whenever they suspected we were doing something they considered deplorable.

"Oh, I'm sure. What are you going to tell them, John? That I'm conversing with commoners?" I snapped.

John straightened his tie and adjusted his suit coat. "Quite the contrary, dear cousin: I will confirm their worst fears! That these *gypsies*—" he spat the word out as if it were disgusting and vile— "brainwashed you, and are trying to convince you to follow in their ways."

"Mother and Father don't care what I do. They never pay me any mind," I replied, trying not to show my uncertainty.

"You're right," he smirked. "But they will when I tell them you've been plotting with your new friends to destroy your father's career."

"Now see here . . ." started Cornelius.

"No, *you* see here, gypsy. You are forbidden from associating with our family," John ordered.

"By who? We have done nothing wrong to Khyra. We have only explained our beliefs," said Freya, Emrys's mother, who was the nicest motherly figure I had ever known.

"My mother is one of the highest-ranking diplomats in the Queen's Parliament! One word from me and rest assured, gypsies, your whole family will regret attempting to poison my impressionable cousin!" John lifted his chin a little higher. He always used his mom as an excuse whenever he knew he was losing an argument, which was almost all the time. His dad was never in the picture—I'm not sure why—but he always seemed to grow tense at the mention of him. I heard my mother and father mention my estranged uncle once or twice, the words *divorced* and *adultery* coming across my young ears, but at the time, I didn't quite understand what they meant.

Emrys, who always seemed to have a better grasp at calming stressful moments, stared at John, trying to figure out the best way to distill the argument. "John, we don't want trouble. If you think it's in the best interest for Khyra to leave, then we will not fight you."

"Perfect! Come along, cousin!" said John, grabbing my arm and dragging me away.

"But," started Emrys. John stopped midstride, waiting to yell at his new enemy. "If your only reason for taking Khyra away is to protect your family's name and ego . . . then I *will* fight you."

For the first time in my life, I saw the egotistical and arrogant John Oak flinch. He'd been called out by a person he deemed beneath him. I wish I could say Emrys fought him and won, but John never retaliated. He stormed away, with me waving goodbye to my only friend. In that moment, I swore I would never forgive John for taking me away. And although I had every intention to reconnect with my old friend, well . . . life decided to take a different turn.

* * *

At first, my lungs felt like they were on fire and a horrendous wheezing replaced my regular breathing. My family believed this sickness stemmed from some rebellious stage, as it came not long after they discovered my friendship with Emrys. But my breathing problems were just the beginning. A harsh fever came rushing over me. It wasn't until I became completely bedridden that my father enlisted the help of every doctor he knew. One right after the other left my room shaking their heads. This crippling sickness was nothing like anything they had ever witnessed in any of their previous patients. What appeared to be a strain of the flu couldn't be weakened by any of man's tested and proven antidotes. At times, I wished the illness would just put me out of my misery, but then there were days when I felt I could fight against its deathly grip. Soon, my sickness became the least of my father's concerns, though. More citizens began reporting a widespread sickness with identical symptoms to my own. And all of those people lived close to a Crawlis Industries plant. I remember lying in bed and sometimes hearing my parents' ongoing arguments, echoing through my partly open door.

"Desmond! Why can't you remove your company's waste in another fashion? There are many other factories that have alternative methods!" said my mother in a hushed whisper.

My father's deep and commanding voice echoed down the hall. "Don't you think I've thought of other ways?"

A hiss followed my father's comment; it was my mother reminding him that voices traveled. I slid out of bed and painfully crawled to my door, straining to hear more of the conversation. My mother replied, "Then perhaps we ought to close Crawlis Industries before anyone else falls ill!"

A low curse escaped my father's lips. "I've worked for far too long and hard to allow a mysterious illness to tear down what I've spent years building!"

"But these are innocent people we're speaking about! Employees, customers, parents, children . . . Desmond! We cannot just put our livelihoods over their—their lives!" stuttered my mom.

Doors creaked open down the hall as the rising conversation woke my siblings. My parents must have noticed, as they took their conversation into the drawing room, but not before I heard my father say the word *cure*.

I wouldn't call his idea a cure, as it seemed more of a way to delay the inevitable. He hired a chemist friend to conduct an experiment on all of those who were sick, one that he claimed would make us better. This chemist always seemed rather shady to me. He claimed he was part of the government, but I suspected the government knew nothing about this chemist or his cure. Even the name of it—Silisk—sounded ominous, and I heard my father say that no one would have to compromise. Meaning it would allow him to continue polluting the environment, and not have to change his usual pattern of operation. Needless to say, it didn't work. No one got better, and my father was forced to cut back on the number of cleaning products his factories produced around the world. Soon we all got better.

My relationship with my father was never close, but we'd never hated each other. That is, until his factories had to change. Several of the products had to be recalled on more occasions than I can remember. It put a massive dent in my father's company funds. I knew getting sick was never my fault; how could it be? But to my father, I was the embodiment of who was to blame. Words were never exchanged, and he didn't express his anger toward me. But there were days when we'd pass by each other in the house and he'd glare at me or even stare in a way that made me feel as if I'd ruined his life.

As for my mother and siblings, they treated me better. My mother saw me as her favorite and my brothers and sister saw me as one of them. I much preferred this over the child that was never meant to be born, a comment my father frequently liked to mention during times I was embarrassing him, to which my mother quickly interjected with, "Oh Desmond, how you love to joke!" She thought her interruption would quell the anger that rose within me, but it didn't. I knew the truth. My father had always detested me and often wished I were never born. But he couldn't blame me for the continuous mistakes he made . . . although he tried. A few times he even blamed me for spreading the sickness to the other citizens, but even my siblings saw through his petty claims. With his family slowly falling out of step with him, my father continued to made mistakes, and he fell into a deep depression that not even his work could pull him from. He was receiving bad publicity, and the press was constantly on him with their conspiracy theories.

Some of his buyers claimed his products had horrific health side effects, while several of his competitors ran slanderous ads, placing my father in an endless battle against them in the courtrooms. I suppose it didn't help that his company conducted most of their business under the table in hopes they wouldn't be shut down. Not to mention all the regulations they broke in creating all these products. I can't count how many people were injured on the job and nothing was reported. Grandfather Lisbon didn't lift a finger to help my father in the least. To him, it was money, and it was my father's job to keep the company upright. If my father didn't deliver on his promise of producing fame and fortune for the family, Lisbon threatened to pull all funding.

For this reason, we moved out of London and set our course for Maine. My father promised us we would one day return to our home country, after the negativity surrounding his work subsided. But even I wasn't that gullible. My father was always boisterous in his opinions and even if what he claimed was true, the negativity would soon return.

The home we settled in happened to be the happiest part of my life, except for my time with Emrys and his family. To this day, I can't recall where in Maine we made our house; somewhere in the north, quite secluded, I suspect. And to my relief it was miles away from my father's factory.

My mother thought our house was quaint compared to the one we'd abandoned in London, but my siblings were appalled that they were forced to downgrade to a country home. It sat on five acres of land, one acre being a beautiful field, which lay behind the house. Tall maple trees surrounded the three-story structure, and a weeping willow draped its branches over one side of it. A form of flowering ivy climbed up the front, giving the building a touch of beauty. To me, this was my long-lost home. Nowhere near civilization, and our closest neighbor lived a quarter mile away. We no longer had the dozens of domestics as we had before, and I liked it that way. I sometimes wondered if I'd lived modestly in another life. The rich and fancy life never suited me, anyway. It was at this point that my family finally saw me as an individual, and not just a cookie-cutter clone of the Crawford clan.

We lived in that house for fifteen years. Richard and Bethany quickly moved out as soon as they were of age, promptly moving back to London. Though they sent letters and eventually transitioned to texting as the years went on, I never saw them again. I believe they went on to be part of the board of directors for Crawlis Industries. Just another step toward their childhood dream—gaining father's fortune. I often wondered if our wealthy grandfather had anything to do with their new position. Then only my brother, Daniel, and I were left. We grew closer when the older two moved out, but we still had our moments of dislike. I suppose it was a normal sibling relationship; at least, that's how I tried to see it.

In the early 2000s, I turned sixteen, and was fortunate enough to graduate high school early. My father flashed all these ivy league college pamphlets in my face, urging me to get a degree of his choosing. That being chemistry or another occupation related to the family business. My mother wasn't as outspoken with her opinions, for which I was truly grateful, but sometimes she kindly hinted at the options my father gave, just to appease him. But I found interests elsewhere. The lessons that Cornelius and Freya taught me about the earth inspired me to learn more about how to protect her. I wanted to become an environmental scientist, but not to rebel against my father's company, although that *was* a plus. I endured my father's constant badgering until I was certain of my choice for university.

To my surprise, Daniel started helping me the most with this transition. Like my older brother and sister, he took a job related to Crawlis Industries, far enough away from the chemicals, but close enough that my father still approved. As we grew closer, Daniel realized I was a hippie at heart, and he didn't want to change that part of me. In some ways, I believe he always liked me, but he couldn't reveal this to Richard and Bethany without being scorned as well.

This change was far from immediate. At first, I didn't trust his new behavior toward me, which is why he did so much for me, to prove that he really cared. He got in touch with as many people as he could and put in a good word for me with some universities. But despite his best efforts, Daniel couldn't protect me from my father's wrath once he discovered my true intentions.

When I spoke to my parents about my dreams, my father believed I was just in a rebellious stage again and would soon see things his way. But when I showed him my many acceptance letters from around the country, the conversation took a dark turn rather quickly.

"How could you do this to me? To us?" exclaimed my father, his face flushed with anger.

"Father, I've always been different from everyone else in this family. I'm sure you've noticed this by now! Is it really a surprise that I chose a different path?" I asked, trying to show him I was mature enough to make this decision.

"Khyra, you're only sixteen. How can you possibly know this is the right path for you?" my father asked, a little kinder.

"I don't know, but how will I if I don't at least explore my options?" I replied, almost pleading.

"Do you realize what this would mean to us? One of my children deliberately going against me? It would appear scandalous, and the media would be in a frenzy!" exclaimed my father, now pacing the living room.

"I never wanted the limelight. I just want a simple life; a life of my own! Why can't I just have that?" I countered.

"Because I forbid it!" my father shouted. "It is not the Crawford way!"

Even the faint pitter-patter of little mice in the kitchen resonated throughout the house as an uncomfortable silence filled the air. My mother, who was sitting on the sofa, put down her needlepoint and stared in horror from me to my father, terrified at who would throw the next verbal blow. My father balled his hands together in tight fists by his side; his body visibly shook in anger. The faded light from the afternoon sun silhouetted him, making him appear fiercer than he was. I remember standing just inside the doorway of our living room, ready to flee should my father start throwing something—this behavior was a recent development.

"No, you mean it's not *your* way." My voice quaked under the weight of my feelings so heavily pent up behind the emotional wall I'd hid behind for all these years. "The *wrong* way, Father."

"Excuse me?" he asked, his face looking rather pale considering the situation.

"You can't force me to become a chemist or take my place in your wretched company!" I exclaimed, standing my ground. I took every acceptance letter in my hand and threw them down at my father's feet. "Every single one of these schools have granted me a full scholarship to attend their universities! All I have to do is choose."

"Sweetheart, how is that possible?" asked my mother, picking up the letters to verify the truth.

"I took all the tests necessary to enter college early and . . . and I had some outside help," I replied, not wanting to reveal Daniel's involvement.

"Khyra, I . . . we've only wanted what's best for you. Please see that!" exclaimed my father.

"Father, not once have you taken any interest in my life. It's always been about the family business. I want no part in it," I replied, feeling my anger from all those years well up within me. "I'd—I'd rather protect Earth than to see her come to ruin by the filthy products you make."

He stared at me coldly. "Well, it appears that you no longer need our assistance. You seem to have everything figured out."

"Desmond!" exclaimed my mother as she jumped to her feet. Her beautiful caramel-colored skin now appeared sickly at the stress of the situation.

"No, Melanie, our daughter is far too mature to need us anymore. It's time she learned how the real world works," he replied, resentment filling his dark brown eyes.

And just like that, my father disowned me. My mother fought him with all she had, short of threatening divorce. Soon word reached Richard and Bethany overseas of my betrayal. Father seemed to think they'd back him up, but they were too self-absorbed in their work to care what nonsense their earth-loving sister had created for herself. Daniel, on the other hand, supported me throughout my college career. What he could give, that was. With his help, and through hard work of my own, I earned a master's degree in environmental toxicology and engineering.

I got a wonderful job as a high school science teacher in Massachusetts while working on my doctorate. Then the tides changed in my life once again at the beginning of 2009. It was a particularly cold that morning, and half of my students either called out sick or were barely keeping their eyes open. I can't say I blamed them; after all, I was only giving a lecture on air pollution. Most of the students stared longingly out the window, possibly wishing that the falling snow would cut the power—giving them a perfect excuse to leave. Just as I was about to call it quits myself, I was interrupted by a knock on the classroom door. Kathleen Rivers, our principal, stood there with a serious expression clouding her usual kind and upbeat disposition. Wordlessly, I nodded to her. I turned my attention back to my students. "Okay, class, we'll continue the rest of our lecture tomorrow. In the meantime, please pay attention to the video I'm about put on." Chatter and giggles spread throughout the room as I popped in the DVD I'd intended for another day. "And I suggest you take notes—there'll be a quiz on it later." I grinned satisfactorily as the students groaned in unison.

After pressing the button to play the movie, I stepped out into the hallway and faced Kathleen. My heart immediately sped up from a rush of anxiety. It seemed we had a special visitor. The man standing at her side wore an expensive black suit and navy-blue tie. The colors perfectly accented his neatly trimmed black hair and bright blue eyes. His five o'clock shadow was barely visible in the fluorescent lights. He was quite attractive, but at this point in my life I had no time for a relationship—at least not a serious one. Silence weighed heavily between all three of us. The man in the suit subtly moved closer to me and glanced at the principal, who stood eagerly, waiting to hear what he had to say. He gave her a curt but dismissive nod. Her face turned a few shades of red as she straightened herself and said, "Oh, I'll leave you to it, then!"

"Thank you, Kathleen." I gave her a kind smile.

Kathleen stared down at the floor as she turned on her heel. She retreaded down the hall with her heavy footsteps echoing on the title, the sounds pinging off the empty walls. She occasionally glanced back, her curiosity obviously still piqued, but likely irritated at not being included in such an apparent secret meeting. As her figure faded, I felt even more anxious in the presence of this stranger.

"Can I help you, Mister . . . ?" I asked.

"Carter, Ms. Crawford. Jonathan Carter. And no, but I might be able to help you. Rumor has it you're working toward earning your doctorate degree. Science. Am I correct?" asked the man, his thick Midwestern accent enunciating each word.

"Perhaps. It depends on who started those rumors," I replied with a smile, hoping he'd receive my jest.

"EWFA Labs, actually," he stated simply, his posture relaxing a little.

"What—how—that's . . . what?" I stuttered, trying to contain my excitement. EWFA Labs— Earth, Water, Fire, and Air Laboratories, to be exact, although sometimes called Balance Labs—were considered the largest environmental science group in almost the entire world. Word around certain circles was they were based in a mysterious location out west. Many of their projects were said to be so top secret, some believed they really dealt with ancient alien life forms. For the longest time, many of my colleagues believed the company to be a myth, yet here I was, witnessing myth as actual reality.

Carter pulled back his suit jacket to reveal the gold encrusted EWFA symbol emblazoned on a badge hanging on a silver chain around his neck. He held it up for me to see his credentials in small print. Seeing I was more convinced of who he claimed to be, Carter allowed his badge to fall back into its place. "We've heard a lot of good things about you, Ms. Crawford. Graduated with all honors from your college, well known, you're the youngest scientist working in the field right now. I'm here on behalf of EWFA to extend an official invitation to our team. We can assist you with your goals."

As excited as I was for this fantastic opportunity, doubt set in quickly, and I could feel my facial expression showing my skepticism.

"If you'd prefer to keep teaching here, I quite understand. Your students are our future, after all." Carter glanced into the darkened classroom.

"No, it's not that. It's ... my father," I replied shamefully.

"Desmond Crawford? You don't have any reason to be worried. Everyone at the lab knows all about the events that transpired to cause you to separate from your father and his company. I must say, you showed great bravery and courage through what you accomplished. You're really respected in the environmental community, Khyra," Carter encouraged me.

Terrible memories flooded my mind at this moment. It took me years to get away from Crawlis Industries. Even when I was in school, I was ridiculed among many of my peers and teachers for rebelling against my father. Many believed he was a great man who wanted to help the world and keep her clean. Then there were others who were absolutely against him, and believed that by my being in the field I was pursuing, I was making a mockery of the environment and those who wanted to keep it free from pollution. They questioned my motives. I struggled to branch out and regain my life—or rather, create it. I eventually gained friends, not a lot, but enough to help pull me from the depression I felt from being a Crawford. I even eventually attended rallies that marched on Crawlis Industries just to prove I wasn't my father's daughter. The media was in a frenzy, and my father went public with his disownment of me. That was probably the only moment in my life that I was grateful for something my father did. But not everyone believed. Then again, people only believe what they wanted to.

In that moment with Mr. Carter, I was unsure if I was beaming after that comment or blushing. I never knew my story had been told, nor even that I had one worth repeating. But I didn't let that go to my head. I didn't need any time whatsoever to ponder my decision in accepting the position. Instead, I agreed to take it, thanked him profusely, and returned to my classroom. Much to my surprise, I walked back in to a round of applause! The movie, which was really a short video clip, had ended, and the students had all gathered near the door to listen in on my private conversation. I probably should've been sterner with them about eavesdropping, but considering how excited they were for me, I found it difficult to scold any of them. Tears emerged as the students gathered around me, cheering for my new endeavor. This was the first time they'd showed interest in me. I suppose I'd made enough of a difference in their lives to warrant such a reaction . . . or I was such a terrible teacher that they were happy to see me go? But in the future weeks, the former option became rather evident. They showed their support of my new adventure by planning and throwing a special going-away party—they even got the whole school together on this. Now, granted, this was a rather small school and news travelled fast. During the party, nearly all the students came up to me with gifts or an expression of gratitude. They all seemed to have had a greater appreciation for Mother Earth than I knew. However, the fact never escaped me that even though this was truly the first time I'd felt like I had a real family, my heart ached in the realization that I had to leave them.

I regret to say my guilt over leaving my students disappeared once I headed out west. Carter was kind enough to travel with me, and given how crazy our journey was, I don't think I could've made it on my own. When we landed in Arizona, I took my two small suitcases and hopped in a black 4x4 vehicle, something Carter called for in advance.

We wound through the desert with only the warm breeze a source of cooling our sweating bodies. I found myself opening up more to this complete stranger, just to fill the time as we drove. I expressed to him more details of my family relations and my education—even Emrys somehow came up in the conversation, although I don't know how.

Carter seemed rather intrigued by the strange Romani boy and asked many questions about Emrys and his parents. I was just feeling myself sinking into that pit of depression, the one that usually came each time I brought up my childhood friend, when Carter suddenly changed the topic and told me a bit about his life. Nothing too dramatic—at least, not like my family. He was an only child, to which I wanted to say "Lucky!" His mother and father supported his dreams of going into politics, and helped him through law school. He quickly climbed the ranks in the political world, and even became a US District Attorney for some time. However, his passion changed course when he discovered the terrible things companies like my father's were doing to the world. Although, that was only half the story. I found out much later, through a bit of research, that his parents were once employed by Crawlis Industries. They believed in a cleaner Earth and tried to steer my father toward that direction, but they were promptly relieved of their duties. Carter never let his true vendetta against the company show too much, although I couldn't help wonder if that's why he created the EWFA Labs. When I discovered he was the founder, I was surprised; Carter looked no older than forty. I was certain the labs had been in existence for much longer, but then again, everything I knew was merely from rumors. I'm sure Carter and I spoke of other things, but my mind soon became too fixated on EWFA Labs and their hidden location. I expected the road to end abruptly and we'd have to hide our vehicle off the road somewhere, but Carter pulled into a parking area designated for hikers. It was at this point I realized I'd missed all the markers for a scenic area. A sign propped up on the side of the road indicated we were at Rincon Mountain and by the looks of it, we weren't the only car in the vicinity. I exited the vehicle in confusion as Carter reached into the backseat to retrieve a large, fully equipped hiking backpack.

"You might want to put your things in the other pack." He gestured to a twin pack next to the one his previously sat next to, only mine appeared less full. "It will look rather odd if you carried your suitcases up the trail, Ms. Crawford," he said nonchalantly, giving me a casual wink.

"To be fair, it'd be odd to have a laboratory at the end of a hiking trail, Mr. Carter," I replied, following his lead. I hastily put my clothes into the pack, suddenly realizing Carter's unusual travel outfit was in fact hiking clothes. I shook my head, silently scolding myself for being unobservant. I guess the mysterious EWFA had diverted my attention from everything. It made me wonder what else I had missed along the way.

Carter smiled as he swung his backpack over his shoulder. "Don't take everything at face value. EWFA Labs is well hidden from the average hiker. Come on, let me show you." He passed by me and began to follow what seemed to be a non-mysterious looking marked trail.

Brushing off this moment, I reluctantly followed after Carter on the trail. I'd never considered myself very athletic, but this trail was unreasonably long and difficult. Hikers passing us on their way down the mountain gave me quizzical side looks. Apparently, my panting and profuse sweating was a clue that hiking wasn't my forte. I tripped over unexpected rocks, almost fell into various ditches—causing me to see my life flash before my eyes at least twice—and I hugged a few trees for balance. It must've taken us at least three or four hours to reach the peak, and still no indication of a secret lab hidden in the mountain. I sat down for a moment to catch my breath while taking in the outstanding view from the top. I grabbed my canteen that came with my pack and took a long swig of water. Carter came over to me and chuckled, as if this situation amused him. I rolled my eyes at the jest, then tilted my head up and squinted. The sun's shining rays streamed brightly into my eyes as my foiled attempted glare at Carter was masked.

"We're almost there, I promise," he assured me, perhaps taking my silence as a sign of irritation.

"Where is 'there' exactly?" I snapped. "This is the end of the trail, there's nowhere else to go!"

"Are you sure about that?" he asked with a sly smile, walking backward toward a cluster of trees.

I rolled my eyes again. He'd only known me for a short period of time, but I always seemed to wear my curiosity on my sleeve. No matter how hard I tried to disguise it under the guise of professionalism, it was something I could never hide. I rose from my resting spot and followed him off the beaten path, where we battled the many branches of the undergrown pine and oak. I followed Carter down a steep incline, and we ended up in a valley between Rincon and Wrong Mountains. From the name of the latter, it seemed like it was intentionally named to misdirect people, possibly from the lab itself.

And as luck would have it, it turned out I was on to something. Just as I asked Carter for what seemed like the hundredth time where he was taking me, he pulled down the branches of a nearby pine tree to reveal a building. The more I studied the architecture, the more I realized it was a laboratory made up entirely of glass.

The building was built in the mouth of a massive cave. Strange, blue-flowered vines that weren't native to the region covered the entrance, concealing a good part of the building. Something told me it was built that way to protect something within the mountain. It wasn't necessarily out in the open for people with binoculars to see, but I'd bet from some floors of the building, neighboring mountaintops could be seen. I'd heard many rumors surrounding the laboratory while I was in college. Area 51 came up quite frequently in some of my classmates' claims. I vaguely remembered something about alien technology and experimentation, or some other such nonsense. At this time, I had no reason to believe in technology outside of what I had learned in classes and seen in other labs. But there were some who said the scientists of the EWFA only answered directly to the president; others said they were conducting experiments to take over the world. It seemed to me the only daunting aspect about this rather clean-looking building was its secrecy.

"Not what you expected?" he asked, noticing my mouth agape.

"Not in the slightest!" I replied, realizing my pack had nearly fallen off my shoulders. "Is this here year-round?"

"Yes. The winter is a bit more challenging, but we try to make do." He walked toward what looked to be the possible entrance into the glass building.

I ran to catch up with him. "Wait, the park rangers don't mind? I mean, don't hikers ever get lost and come across this place?"

"Not easily, no. Besides, the 'park rangers' work for us. Anyone who comes across our laboratory suddenly finds themselves back on the main trail . . . and coincidentally confused as to how they got there," he replied mischievously.

"So it's true—you only report to the president?" I asked, hoping to dispel some myths.

"We don't report to anyone. We only announce our findings to certain individuals, and that's only because those individuals and EWFA Labs have a common vested interest." He took out a badge to open the front door. "Any rumors you might've heard are just that: rumors. We're about as elusive as aliens."

"*Jonathan Carter*," announced a disembodied voice as the door slid open with a *swoosh*. I stared at Carter and laughed. "You're not saying aliens exist . . . are you?"

"Ask me that after I give you the tour," he replied with a knowing smile.

We stepped into the entryway of the building as a robotic female voice echoed all around us: "Please wait for decontamination." A strange, odorless vapor swept over us and the next door opened, welcoming us to the facility.

"Are you really sure this is EWFA Labs?" I said between coughs. "And what was in that mist?"

He looked back at the entrance and understood my concern completely. "Oh, that's an invention of our own making. We used all natural materials. Everything you see here and beyond was created for the sole purpose of protecting our discoveries. We can't let anything from the outside world contaminate what we're working on. From the structure itself to the automated doors, we're keeping the future of our planet in mind. Now follow me; I have much to show you!"

I willingly followed Carter through the laboratory as he pointed out white and silver colored machines that lined the walls of the rectangular room. Most of them were barely the height of a man. Technicians stood in front of these inventions, pressing buttons of small panels and reading out the results. In the middle of the room stood tables and desks, each one lining the room in two neat rows. It all appeared rather symmetrical, as if someone with a serious case of OCD designed the layout. Biologists, ecologists, botanists, and many more sat at these desks and tables— each one clustered based on their varying degrees. I was so amazed at my surroundings that I forgot Carter had been speaking to me for much time. Fortunately, I was able to catch the last bit of information regarding EWFA, "All of these were created and designed from recycled pieces from other various machines. They've proven to be more efficient than their counterparts on the market. This immediately proves what we as a company seek to do here."

The living quarters were on the upper floors, as were the dining halls—the levels could all be seen from the ground floor. A grand staircase led up to the first floor and continued up to the third and final level of the facility. Looking straight up, each had its own landing, which overlooked the bottom floor. I expected there was a great view of the surrounding scenery from the top. Every hallway was stripped of décor; all that remained were the pristine white walls and shiny tiles. In some ways, it resembled what I'd always imagined an insane asylum would look like. Even the living quarters looked the same—a combination of grey and white, and some of the open doors revealed that the other scientists hadn't brought many of their worldly possessions.

I supposed the work here took up most of their interest. When I mentioned this to Carter, he said only a dozen scientists worked and lived here, including myself. They chose to bring only a few things, as they didn't want to be distracted by memories of their former life. It was as if this laboratory acted as some kind of religious sanctum. *My* reasoning for bringing just a select few items was because I didn't own a lot—well, enough to care about, anyway. Seeing my future colleagues' dedication was quite amazing, but my mind remained stuck on the group's discoveries and what was so important that I needed to have a vapor shower upon entering. That's when he led me to the back door of the facility. He pulled out his badge from his jacket pocket and placed it in front of a small box. The disembodied voice echoed his name once more as the door slid open. A blast of cool, fresh air blew past me as I followed him down a long tunnel, dark save for muted solar-powered lights along the way.

I found myself speechless yet again as we turned the last corner and entered into what seemed like another world. A massive cove loomed close in the distance, with a small pond to its side that contained stunningly clear water. Absentmindedly, I walked closer to the crystal water, almost mesmerized by its beauty. The soft grass beneath my feet felt like memory foam, as if the earth were trying to remember who I was. I stared into the transparent surface and knelt down to touch it, to see if it was even real. The water itself felt smooth and warm, almost unnatural. Rocks of various sizes jutted up from the water—their submerged parts appearing a vibrant blue in contrast with their gray, dry tops. I assumed it was due to the blue algae covering the bottom of the pond. I noticed biologists and hydrologists working together near the far edge taking water samples and conversing quietly amongst themselves. Vibrant grass covering the ground around the pond looked even healthier than the lush rolling hills covering Ireland. In rare spots where dirt was exposed, it appeared to be the cleanest and purest soil I had ever seen. And don't get me started on the air: I can't even explain how free of pollution it was. I smelled nothing, but it felt comfortably cool and fresh, almost like mountain air.

"Beautiful, isn't it?" asked Carter, breaking me from my amazement. "It's the last place on Earth that hasn't been touched by mankind."

"How is that even possible?" I asked.

"We don't know exactly—it's as if Earth wants us to fight back against mankind. And that's what we're trying to do. All the samples taken from this cove are intended to be used against air, water, and soil pollution. So far, we've done a pretty good job," Carter explained.

"What do you mean, 'good job'? What all have you discovered?" I asked, turning my full attention to him.

"Well, your father has been a great subject for us," Carter mused. "Throughout the years we've been taking elemental samples near his factories and tested them here. We've been able to come up with solutions that have, at the moment, an eighty-five percent success rate of cleaning the environment around these locations."

"How can you use the elements to reduce pollution— that hasn't been . . . that can't be done," I replied, reflecting back on all my studies from college 'til now.

"I understand your skepticism. Believe me, I had doubts at first too! But we've been creating solutions for years and emitting them into larger populated areas. It took us a very long time to convince the government to allow us to do that. But it has no effect on people or animals, except for clearing the air and making water fresher. Although you probably wouldn't have noticed much of a difference, as we're restricted to certain cities," said Carter.

"So where do I come in? You seem to have a good handle on things."

Carter hung his head low, as if he wished I hadn't asked that question. He shook his head and looked up. "We've been keeping an eye on your dad, of course, as he runs one of the biggest pollution-making companies in the entire world. For years he was . . tolerable, but recently he's been up to something that we can't quite understand. We were hoping *you* could find out what it is he's doing differently."

"Wait: you want me to spy on my father? Is that the only reason you asked me to join your team? You want to *use* me?" I was taken aback.

The scientists who'd been taking samples were now staring at me and Carter—apparently, I hadn't been as quiet as I'd thought. Carter glanced at the others and nodded, giving them a rather shaky smile. They returned to their work, their conversations now more audible.

Carter looked rather uncomfortable at the tension in the air. He'd no doubt purposefully left this little bit of information out in the hopes that the facility and their goals would inspire me to agree without hesitation. "Khyra, you're the only one who can get around your father. You must have some kind of connection with your mother, or maybe your siblings."

All my life I'd been used by my family—for blame, or anything else they'd seen as useful—and here I was in my own environment, being used again. To say I was annoyed was an understatement: I was furious. At myself for constantly getting in situations like this; at my family for ingraining this type of behavior into my brain. I knew this position with EWFA Labs would provide me the doctorate I needed, and I *couldn't* go back to teaching all I'd seen here so far.

I had to find out more about what Carter meant about Crawlis Industries. I looked at him and grudgingly replied, "I'll see what I can do."

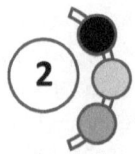

2

I called the only person in my family who I knew had ears everywhere and could possibly give me any inside details—Daniel. My fingers trembled in anticipation as I pulled up his number and hit *call*. He picked up within the first couple of rings. I laid out my concerns regarding my father's factories . . . and, well, Daniel didn't take it kindly.

"What're you talking about? Father's facilities have hardly emitted any pollution since you were younger. What makes you think he reverted back? It's unethical and damaging to his company's already tarnished reputation if this is true. Where did you get this information?"

I stood in the cool shade of the cave outside the laboratory as I spoke to my brother. My creeping rush of anxiety kicked into full gear. I began to pace to compensate. I remembered plenty of nights throughout my childhood catching sight of my father doing the same. His feet had made a soft padding noise with each anxious step. I brought myself back to the present and mentally debated over how much of a wrong turn this conversation was taking.

There are times when you wish your older siblings saw your side of things and agreed with you, no questions asked. Clearly, Daniel was anything but convinced. "I—I don't exactly know." I paused. "There are rumors—"

"Rumors?" he cut in, immediately sounding skeptical.

"Yes, rumors have risen within the environmentalist community regarding Crawlis Industries. I know nothing more than that."

"Then perhaps they are just that. Rumors. Believe me, if Father was conducting more experiments, the world would know, and you'd be the first person I'd tell. But I haven't heard anyth—" His reply broke into a series of harsh coughs, and his breathing grew ragged as he tried to settle himself down.

"Are you all right? That cough doesn't sound good," I replied, thinking the conversation was upsetting him.

"I've had the flu for a while—don't worry about me; it's been going around up here. Just keep focused on working on your doctorate. Stop worrying about what Father is doing. If any news regarding him comes up, I'll handle it. It's my responsibility, not yours. You have enough on your plate as it is. Goodbye, Khyra," Daniel's now raspy voice whispered, and he abruptly hung up.

I sighed and felt my head ache from the stress of the situation. I leaned my head against one of the walls of the cave. Its natural coolness crept into the base on my skull and made its way to my temples. Its natural temperature seemed to be the best medicine at this moment. My mind proceeded to rewind back to the conversation.

Daniel was right, much as I hated to admit it. I had no reason to suspect my father of any suspicious activity, at least at this time. But there was something eating at me, something I couldn't fight. My father had never forgiven me from the past, nor had he ever fully seemed set on the idea of changing. My intuition held on tight, like a child onto her mother's legs when meeting strangers for the first time. There were times when I was a young girl when I'd heard my mother plead to my father to alter certain ways he ran the company, but he'd stood firm in what he was doing.

I just knew these rumors would either grow more radical—or worse, be proven true.

Then there was the matter of Daniel's illness. It was troubling. He was always the healthiest person in our family. I could count on one hand throughout our lives when he'd barely had anything worse than a common cold.

I shook my head and breathed in the clear, fresh air from the cave. The more I stood in its presence, the more my anxiety faded into darkness. I had to put it aside as soon as possible and meet Carter for our three o'clock appointment. I glanced at my watch, a going-away present from my former students. It reminded me that they were still out there, studying and pursuing their dreams to someday be where I was at that very moment. I wouldn't let them—or anyone else—down, and more importantly, myself above all. The hands maneuvered to five minutes 'til, and I made my way back into the lab's conference room. Like much of the facility, it had pristine tile flooring, and the room was immaculate. It contained neither art nor beauty, save the white flowers displayed as a centerpiece in the middle of the long, rectangular gray table in the center of the room. Several empty chairs sat around it, with only Carter sitting at the head. This particular room made me a bit nervous, as it stood at the top of the building, with windows instead of walls. It was certainly beautiful, but not for someone with a fear of heights, which sadly, I had.

Shaking off my fear, I sat down in a chair closest to Carter and briefed him on my short conversation with Daniel. Carter didn't give any indication of disappointment in his face, but his shoulders slumped a little before he shook it off.

"No matter, I have another assignment for you instead." He cleared his throat. For a moment, my mind flashed back to the previous evening's events. He'd revealed his suspicions of my family's business practices while we'd taken a stroll in the lab gardens. He finally came to me with the truth about his family's dealing with Crawlis Industries, just validating what I researched. He believed that Crawlis Industries was conducting harmful experiments, at least more than what the world already suspected. I then questioned where he obtained this information. In turn, he cast his eyes away from mine and declared it classified under government privacy protocol.

I'd never fully trusted my adopted country's government, due to obviously deceitful and self-serving practices—and not just pertaining to environmental safety measures. Call me a believer in conspiracy theories or a crackpot for what I believed our government was capable of doing, but we were standing in a location that was considered *nonexistent* to the public, and a mere conspiracy theory in and of itself—literally.

Carter cleared his throat, bringing me back to the present. "I need you to travel to Tucson and take some samples there to test them against the pure elements from the cove."

I cocked my head to the side, crossing my arms. "Really? With all due respect, I've spoken to Sarah and Hank. They've already taken several samples from there, specifically saying it's the closest polluted city to our laboratory."

Carter's tired eyes close for a second, as if he were trying not to lose his temper. Why would he? I didn't know, but I wasn't going to waste valuable time when we should be working on other projects.

He placed his hands on the meeting table and opened his eyes. His stare held a mix of sympathy clouded with exhaustion and desperation. "Unfortunately, Sarah and Hank's samples didn't contain enough pollution. Tucson, although it is heavily populated, doesn't have enough of Crawlis Industries' pollution. I have found there to be some select areas around a few of the companies that carry or use Crawlis products. But it's the closest we can feasibly get to the company without arousing suspicion. Khyra, you are one of the best scientists we have here. Just do your research and . . . find something we can use." With that, I was dismissed and carted away to Tucson with two other scientists as my companions.

Six hours of watching our backs, rising temperatures, and a cooler full of samples later, we returned to the glass building. I retreated to my work area in the main lab space to find a wrinkled letter sitting on my workbench. My childhood home address was scrawled at the top left corner of the envelope, and judging by the shaky handwriting, it was from my mother. I pulled the letter out, her familiar perfume wafting into my nose, and a faded smile crossed my face.

My mother despised technology and always preferred to do things the old-fashioned way if she could help it. Somehow, she'd found out my new mailing address, probably through Daniel, who came to his senses about Crawlis Industries' corruption. Although he still worked for them along with my other siblings on the board of directors. Daniel acted as our insider to the company and became the only person directly authorized from the head of EWFA himself to know certain specific details of my occupation.

His contribution to our cause also placed him in good favor with EWFA. Quite often, he would send us anonymous donations through our post office box. Only myself and the head of the labs knew who was being so generous.

The beginning of my mother's letter was just small updates about things happening in Maine. New people had moved into the neighborhood, and they had small children. She reminisced about memories when my siblings and I were young as well—I suppose there were moments during that time that she found peaceful. But the further down I read, the darker its contents became. Mother went into detail over father's business—she must have shared this without his knowledge.

"I know you would rather not hear about this," her letter began, "but I'm very worried about your father. By now I'm sure you've heard about all the rumors flying about regarding Crawlis Industries' pollution. But that isn't why I'm writing to you..."

I skimmed through my mother's ramblings to find the more interesting parts of her letter as it continued, "I overheard him the other day speaking with an investor. I didn't quite catch everything, but I heard enough to know that there is this report that your father is spending an awful lot of money trying to hide. Could it be true, Khyra? Could these rumors have any merit to them? This is rather silly of me to be concerning you, as you have previously stated that you want nothing to do with the company. I don't even know why I'm bothering to send you this letter. I suppose its because your brothers and sister will not listen to me. I just am not sure what we are going to do as the amount of money your father mentioned to the investor is far from what we can afford. Have you heard anything? If so, please let me know, I can't bare the thought of our lives being ruined over a foolish decision!"

My heart sped up after the closing of the letter and I knew I had to inform Carter right away of my mother's news. I rushed to Carter's office and knocked on the glass door. The moment he opened it, I thrust the letter at him and told him to read it. A smiled tugged at the corner of his lips and grew impossibly wide to have evidence of these rumors being true. But now, the true challenge: How were we going to prove it? It certainly wasn't going to be easy, especially if my father ever caught wind of what we were doing. His investors obviously knew what *they* were doing, and they had lawyers at their disposal to throw even more shade at our claims if we ever brought them to the public. I shuddered at the thought of headlines rolling out over these findings.

Despite my worries, Carter immediately went to work at uncovering the evidence behind my mother's words. We put in countless hours and tests, looking for support to back up my mother's claims, but without a way into my father's facilities, we were fit to be tied. My father and his crew knew how to cover their tracks—not only with heightened security, but by making sure victims were paid for their silence. We only discovered this through our informant, an eager reporter whose friends and family were also wronged by Crawlis Industries. He found his way into the company and used his cell phone to record secret meetings and also cleverly intercepted many letters. In my opinion, he should have been a P.I. versus a reporter, but then again, oftentimes they are one in the same. Now, to a normal person our informant's findings would seem rather suspicious, but any jury presented this case would only consider our accusations as hearsay and, obviously, rumors. Not to mention our findings were technically illegal, if anything they just stirred our anger even more. I have to give some credit to the judge presiding over this case. He initially took pity on us and ordered samples to be taken at Crawlis Industries and in the various locations. But by some unknown miracle, my father escaped through our clutches again. We have no idea what samples were taken and where, but I guarantee they were not from the factories as the results were free of any contaminants. To make matters worse, when we argued this in court, the judge threw it out, his sympathy for our plight diminishing. The odds continued to stack against us. Since I was part of EWFA Labs, the jury began casting their stones upon me, considering I was a former victim, probably mad that my father had disinherited me, and seeking revenge. Carter, though, would not give up without a fight. Six months later, the press caught wind of the investigation. Seeing father pitted against daughter, you'd think the media had found their personal Holy Grail! It was disgusting.

When the judge dismissed the case a few months later, everyone went home free of any charges. That is, until my father ended up suing us for some emotional trauma nonsense. Did it put a dent in our funding? Most definitely, but it didn't tear us down in the least. We still had funding from Daniel and a few anonymous corporations who believed in our mission within the government. But I think the most damage it did was preventing us from getting closer to uncovering the truth. We had no choice but to walk away from it all, but believe me, we still fought back in our own way.

I conversed with my mother through occasional letters and phone calls. I always used a fake name when writing in order to divert attention, and the information she provided in return was truly valuable to us. She saw my father growing even angrier as the days progressed, and it terrified her. But there was nothing she could do except secretly protest against him by providing insight where we had none.

She spoke of situations other states were facing. More and more people were reporting cases of a virus that seemed to infect the lungs to a dangerous degree. However, I couldn't stand by as a mere observer any longer when she finally told me the identity of one such victim: Daniel.

I gripped the letter containing this news with a deep anger I never knew existed. My brother Daniel, one of our main supporters in our fight. Daniel, who never gave up on me and always stood by me. As the anger seeped deeper into my veins, my mind took over in searching for ways to help us end the war on pollution.

Through many connections and calling in various favors. Due to a very daring intern, I managed to get my hands on a sample of the water and air retrieved around one of the Crawlis Industries locations closest to the lab. Countless hours were spent testing and searching. Test tubes with collected data were sprinkled about the majority of the lab. Our conclusions—well, that was nothing we were prepared for. The pollution seemed to have a mind of its own. What came from Crawlis Industries was an entity of which none of our toxicity reduction solutions were effective against. It was like ... a monster. A monster that continuously evolved through time, ever-changing to battle every solution we tried.

"We've exhausted all our resources and time. We have no choice. I think it's time we deliver our research to the public," said Sarah Martin, one of the main scientists attached to the project.

"Sarah, we still don't know what chemicals this pollution consists of. I believe it'd be in everyone's best interest if we did more research," I replied, rubbing my eyes from lack of sleep.

"And then what?" asked Carter slightly irritable, "What's more research going to do, Khyra? Sarah's right, we're out of time. Perhaps if we did tell the public, someone out there can come up with a solution that our resources can't!"

"I think we might be rushing it—" I started.

"So, we wait for it to kill someone?" Sarah interrupted. "For all we know that may have already happened, but was covered up!"

As if on cue, Hank, the oldest scientist, strolled in with the mail and handed me another letter from my mother. I immediately rushed to open it, quickly scanning it. My hand shook under the weight of it as I finished. "M-my father and brother, Daniel, are dead."

The letter fell to the floor and the room slowly spun around me. I lifted my eyes to Carter, who seemed to be the only one in the room not moving.

"I'm sorry. I know how close you were to Daniel," said Carter.

"Well, this poses as another problem." Andrea, who was a new intern, spoke up from the other side of the room. "Now who is to inherit and control Crawlis Industries?"

"My grandfather passed away a few years prior, leaving my father as the sole proprietor of the company. But as far as I know, my father never specified who was to inherit his business in his will—or at least, my mother hasn't said as much," I said.

Carter took back control of the conversation. "This is it, now's the time to expose Crawlis for what they're doing— we can do it in coordination with the news that its pollutants have killed two of their own!"

So, in that spring of 2011, Crawlis Industries came under fire by the media. The investors missed one man who suffered from this strange new illness, who brought his case to the local news stations. Just like that, all previous qualms involving former victims were resurrected, taking the company down, and production was immediately shut down under government order. Since there was no legally established heir to the company throne, though, it was unclear who should take the reins and handle the turmoil . . . and the blame. Due to the confusion, the company automatically fell into the laps of Richard and Bethany, who were more than happy to take over— naturally. Without Daniel as our insider, we had a challenging time trying to get news from inside Crawlis' fortress. Surprisingly, my late brother gained a secret following of workers from within the company before he passed. They carried on his task of keeping us informed about the factory. And let me say, if Karma exists, my older siblings certainly got what was coming to them. They struggled to maintain order within the company, not to mention the media frenzy. Soon, their television appearances became fewer and fewer to the point where everyone wondered where they were. According to our new informants, Richard and Bethany secretly liquidated the company, their promises of making the company better and finding solutions to the sick were found to be empty. They robbed the company dry causing thousands of people to be out of work. As for the chemists who worked with Crawlis, they were divided. Some joined forces with my siblings and those with morals fought valiantly against their corruption, but to no avail. This essentially was the end of my father's legacy. Richard and Bethany split their stolen money and fled to different parts of the globe. I never knew where their new residence ended up being, and I honestly didn't care. They single-handedly did the one thing EWFA Labs had been trying to do for years. Although Crawlis Industries' factories lay abandoned, their terrible pollutant did not. It was quickly given the name the Toxin and began mutating once again on its own by August. Looking back, I wish we could've done something sooner, but we had very little room or proof to do anything. Panic set in worldwide and not even Hollywood could've predicted the mass hysteria that ensued.

Robberies, fights, and protesters started casting blame about the outbreak at the closest groups of people they could find. Governmental officials, most of them holed up in their homes, operated their meetings through the underground trying to figure out a possible solution. And while those who were still healthy stayed holed up at home, terrified of catching the sickness, infected bodies dropped right and left on the streets. By six months, cemeteries around the globe were filled, and mass cremation became a necessity. The stench alone was enough to kill a man. Sometimes it did. But even worse, the smoke from the cremation released more toxicity into the air. This, in turn, greatly affected the wildlife as they began to drop in numbers too. Life without the chirping of birds or squabbles of arguing squirrels seemed rather empty.

Under governmental authority, EWFA Labs was ordered to do everything in its power to come to the aid of those affected by the illness. We ceased all of our research and used some of the elements from the cover to help those who were affected. Most of our aid went to surrounding hospitals and, in some cases, we managed to contain elements from the cove to be transported to different states. It acted as a bandage for the affected, but it only helped prolong their lifespan.

Only three percent of the world's population remained by February 21, 2012. Parks were empty. Playground equipment lay rusting in their wake, waiting for the children that would never come. Restaurants too, lay barren, except for the occasional rodent feasting on the rotting food in the kitchens or human remains. Those who were still alive left store shelves empty, yet another sign of fleeting hope. The major news stations remained in operation until reporters began dying onscreen. And just when life couldn't get worse, it did. The world's leading authorities, or what remained of them, banded together and formed what they called *The Great Merge*.

Terrorists gained control of the Middle East, although some smaller countries withdrew support and isolated themselves when they got wind of their enemies' plans. The people of South Korea fled to nearby countries sometime in May 2012. Two months later, North Korea's government fell completely. I don't know if anyone managed to escape the continual chaos wreaking havoc in the region. In the fall of the same year, the island countries merged. Taiwan's government joined with the Philippines. All small countries between Mexico and South America divided and spread to their nearest perspective continents. North America and South America feuded over this plan. I would say Haiti and Puerto Rico got lucky and didn't get involved, but that was because they no longer existed.

By Halloween of 2012, no self-governing island country existed anymore. Within two months, the continents of North America, South America, and Africa became their own singular, massive countries. Australia and New Zealand citizens moved up to Asia, although not a lot of people made the trek successfully. Europe and Asia, through a lot of fighting, ended up agreeing to merge, mostly to save their populations. Greenland, however, was another country that sadly didn't make it. They were too isolated, and had shut down their borders when the Toxin first broke, effectively shutting themselves off from flight or rescue.

June came around and we were all finally coexisting.

When the first reporter died on air, the media banded together to create an alternative broadcast in case they could no longer deliver the news through normal means. This quickly became the case as the latest technology became unusable. Each continent had two main radios. One radio was dedicated to communicating to the different continents while the other was strictly within each continent. The global radio sent radio messages to each other via Morse code. When the messages were received it was then translated into words and distributed to the continental radios which nearly every citizen had in their home, and if not, they could easily go to the town hall to receive said messages. This was a similar set up to that of the emergency broadcast system from back in the mid to late 1900s. What made these two radios different from all others was how they were powered. Solar panels were connected to pre-existing radio towers and gave these radios the juice they needed to work. Now, messages were sent every so often, though sometimes they were met with static or were completely cut off. So, the messages had to be absolutely accurate before sending, as each transmission drained power, and the radio would take at least a week to recharge, maybe more. Strategically placed solar panels were placed in a way so that it constantly charged the already-standing radio towers. The towers that were chosen were not selected at random, but in a way that everything could eventually be connected. But what seemed like a possible fix would only last until February 7, 2014, when our lives changed again.

* * *

"Just turn off the radio—I can't take any more bad news," said Carter exasperatedly, rubbing his hands over his stubble-ridden face.

Only Carter and I, and a handful of other scientists, remained at EWFA Labs at this point. Our hopes of helping the citizens of Arizona and the surrounding states had quickly diminished, as most of them were dead. The days at the laboratory grew depressing, and we had no way of helping our fellow scientists find a cure for this plague. We tried examining the sick to see if there was a connection to regular flu-type symptoms. But any medication we gave them or even altered seemed only to enhance their illness. Really, we were just staying in the laboratory until we died as well. But I still had some hope, which is why I often had the radios going. I knew there was hardly ever any good news, but within the last few days I swore I'd heard something different than just the codes.

"I think someone is trying to add another code, Carter. It was a series of numbers," I explained, playing with the dials of the crudely built machine.

"It's probably some kind of interference from an old signal. Besides, who'd want to tell the world a bunch of numbers?" Carter replied.

"But that's not all." I motioned to the sounds echoing through the speakers. "There! I'm sure I caught another word before the numbers . . . it was just really faint."

"We all want some kind of miracle, Khyra, but a hidden message from the radio? That's . . . that's just reaching," Sarah interjected from a cot on the floor in the corner of the lab.

Just as Sarah and Carter rose and turned to leave the room, one word echoed from the machine and bounced off the glass walls of the empty laboratory.

"*Hope.*"

Sarah and Carter turned just as the numbers came through. I grabbed for a pen and jotted the instructions down on my arm, almost running out of room. Sarah and Carter came back and studied the numbers. I looked up at them with excitement: this could very well be something new in our desolate world.

"Okay, so you got a word and numbers—now what do we do?" asked Carter, sounding skeptical.

I stared at the numbers, expecting the answer to jump out at me, but I still didn't understand. I shook my head and replied, "Now, we solve the mystery."

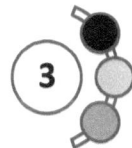

3

This wasn't as easy as I'd expected. With only numbers to work with and obviously no other instructions given, understanding the cipher was nearly impossible. And that four-letter word, hope, haunted us every day, even without the helpful reminder from our radio. I eventually shut it off. Staring at it in the dead silence felt like it was teasing me more than anything. There were days like these where I second-guessed my efforts. What if this was some kind of scam? Or, like Carter suggested, interference? But at the same time, the global radio had only one channel, and as far as I knew, no other radio on the planet was as powerful as the one sending the codes.

Unfortunately, my research into these mysterious numbers was put on hold when Sarah and Carter, the last of the team, succumbed to the sickness in a matter of weeks and quickly passed away. As for Sarah, I mourned her in my own way as we became good friends over time. But Carter. His last few weeks were the most difficult time of my life. It was as if I lost Daniel all over again, although Carter's death seemed more drawn out in a strange way. This was the Toxin's way of mocking me. At least, that's what it felt like. Carter's hacking and terrible cold sweats haunted my memory after his passing and only made me strive harder to decipher the elusive message. I owed it to him to follow through on my theory.

I was now officially alone, but I felt I owed it to my colleagues to solve this bizarre mystery. After all, it was my idea to focus on this puzzle. They could've left, but they'd been loyal to me and believed I was onto something despite being skeptical at the same time.

Yet with no lead on this mystery, doubt began creeping back in. I wondered why I was left alive, figuring it was some sort of cosmic joke. By the middle of April, I was on my last straw. The numbers were making no sense, and I didn't exactly have internet capability to find more information. With everything that had happened in the last few months, I momentarily lost it and became so angry that I threw all my research off my desk. Tears streamed down my face as I finally resigned to dying in this glass coffin, depressed and alone. I wished the disease had taken me first.

Staring unfocused around the room, a flash of light caught my eye. In front of my massive window, left completely forgotten, stood a massive globe covered in a thick coat of dust due to years of disuse. I walked over to the antique and blew off the dust. The image of a map of the United States mocked me, and that's when I noticed the lines traced evenly through the continent, signifying longitude and latitude coordinates.

The numbers! They were coordinates! I scrambled to the mass of papers lying scattered on the floor and dug through the pile to find my original numbers. Grabbing the globe, I placed it next to the papers. My heart raced as my finger traced the lines on the globe, following the direction of the numbers. I narrowed down my search to part of the world, but then I shook my head in irritation. These were coordinates, but without an exact location. Those numbers could send me to two different areas of Antarctica, or off the coast of Alaska, or some remote place in northeast Siberia, all of which couldn't be possible.

My months of research had finally gotten me somewhere, and I was really excited, but now I had to make educated guesses about where I was supposed to go. I also had to take into consideration that I had no idea what I was looking for, or if what Sarah had said was true—I may have been reaching after all. Since no one had sent a science team to Antarctica for many years, those two possible locations could be logically ruled out. I had only Alaska and Siberia to consider. And since the latter was too far away, I based my decision on practicality. I packed what little I had and made my way to the coast of Alaska in the hope that someone there had the right answer.

My journey was not easy. I had no car and there weren't a lot of vehicles on the road anyway, so I hiked into the nearest town and was fortunate enough to find a store with camping gear. There were times I was able to hotwire an abandoned vehicle. Moments like those, I was grateful for my rebellious stages in my youth. I'd learned how to hotwire a car whenever I wanted to escape from my father's suffocating watch. Though my efforts, as I vaguely recalled, had been futile, as he'd somehow managed to catch me in the act every time.

The rush of hotwiring a car only lasted for so long on my lengthy journey. Many of the vehicles I stole had either a half a tank of gas or very little at all. Many times I resorted to walking.

Getting to Alaska took almost two months—that's including the breaks and detours I had to take. Fortunately, I could freely travel through the old Canadian territory without any hassle, as Canada and America were now one country.

Sometime around the middle of June, I found myself in Anchorage, Alaska. The gorgeous snow-covered mountains loomed in the distance, the large city sitting in the shadows. As I roamed the streets, I felt as if I were in some apocalyptic movie. Not a soul was in sight as random garbage blew across my path in the warm breeze. Occasionally I'd duck into some stores to change clothes or grab any remaining food I could find on shelves in a few abandoned markets. Fortunately, Anchorage was large enough were I found a few essential items left in some smaller shops. I found a hotel near the port and camped there for the night.

A loud horn woke me up at the crack of dawn. Thinking it to be some faulty alarm system, I ignored it and tried getting more sleep, but then it went off again. I propped myself on my elbows and focused on the sound. It wasn't an alarm at all, but a ship's horn. I rushed over to my room's window. It was a massive vessel at that. My fifth-story window gave me the perfect view of the city and the distant ocean. With the sun just peering over the mountains, it seemed to put a spotlight on the biggest ship I had ever seen. It sat idle about five miles out as small passenger boats dotted the waters.

I quickly changed and gathered my things together. The sun greeted me upon my exit out of the building as I followed a trail leading back to the port, which was practically below me. And that's when I heard it: the sweetest sounds ever to reach my ears. Voices. At first, I thought I had lost my mind, but then I saw small figures surrounding the docks, getting ready to ship off to some unknown land. I started running toward them.

Just the thought of civilization surpassed all doubts I'd had of surviving this soon-to-be ghost world. My legs felt like jelly as I ran the few blocks to the water's edge. In fact, I received several strange looks by the time I reached the group of people. Some looked pleased to see an outsider, while others seemed to view my abrupt arrival as rather odd. I scanned the crowd, looking for the person in charge of what I believed to be a voyage.

"Antarctica or Siberia?" came a female voice from behind me.

The woman's voice shook me out of my stupor. I turned to see a young Asian woman holding a clipboard. Her fine black hair was pulled back in a ponytail, and her clothes were rather worn. I stuttered: "W-what . . . where?"

"Are you traveling to Antarctica or Siberia?" the woman asked impatiently.

"What's the difference?" I asked, still confused about the two locations.

She threw her head back and heaved an unnecessarily loud sigh before shouting, "Oscar! Got a newbie!"

A southern accent erupted from a big, burly man emerging from the crowd: "Thank ya, Lian, I'll take it from here."

He walked with a limp and his large beer belly jiggled underneath his oversized, stained shirt, his suspenders threatening to burst under all his weight. His scruffy black beard was laced with strands of gray and his dark blue eyes appeared like small buttons above his pudgy red cheeks.

"Forget Lian; she deals with stress differently than the rest of us. I'm Oscar. What's your name?" he introduced himself, cheerfully extending a hand the size of my face.

"Uh . . . Khyra," I replied uncertainly, taking his kind gesture and grasping his hand.

"Khyra, nice to have you on board! Tell me, where ya headed?" He gestured to two ships that were already taking passengers.

"I don't know, actually," I replied as my brows furrowed, trying to understand their operation. "This might sound kind of crazy, but I came here by coordinates through the global radio."

Oscar's cheery disposition faded as soon as I gave him my explanation, his tone now quite serious. "Ah, so you're one of 'em? I'm not gonna even bother convincing you to go to Antarctica. Seems everyone one of you 'radio folk' are goin' to the same place. Take the boat headed to Siberia. But don't ever expect to come back. Nothin but wasteland up there now."

I looked at the boatful of people who now struck me as having an intellectual air about them. They seemed nervous, but not as terrified as the people in the boat headed to Antarctica. I turned back to Oscar who was pushing his way through the crowd. Wanting to know more about *his* future home and what he knew, I asked, "Oscar, how do you know Antarctica isn't wasteland too?"

"'Cause all of them scientist people are down there, and have been figurin' stuff out in their labs. Rumor has it they've discovered a way to clean the earth of this toxic stuff," he replied, probably trying to sound smart.

I just silently nodded, knowing the truth: they were heading straight for their deaths. Suggesting this to the group of Antarctica voyagers would have been pointless. They were all afraid and if I gave away who I was, that'd start a potential riot, one I wouldn't get out of alive. With a sorrowful heart, I made my way toward the Siberian voyage and we soon cast off to our ship in the ocean, leaving America behind. We sped through the waters, past the large boat I had seen from my hotel window, and steamed off toward the Gulf of Alaska.

Just off the edge of what looked to be some kind of nature preserve sat the largest ship I'd ever seen. I didn't know much about seafaring vessels, but I could easily tell this wasn't just a typical cruise ship. This was some kind of double-acting tanker, one that could travel through water and ice. These people really did their homework on where we were going, and my confidence rose as we boarded the vessel. My only question was where, exactly, were we headed? The voyage took about two weeks to complete, but at times it felt much longer. Along the way we encountered other ships: some going in our direction, allowing us to take the lead; but then there were others, like the ones back in Anchorage who believed their hope lay within the barren land of Antarctica.

The lengthy trip was one matter, but the struggles we endured were a whole different story. We were well into our voyage when people grew sick, not just from the Toxin, but also from other illnesses such as pneumonia, hypothermia, and in some rare cases gangrene. Many people died and soon many of the boats in our growing fleet had a mass sea burial, sending at least a thousand people to their watery graves. I didn't know any of the deceased personally, but the ongoing losses were a constant reminder of the environmental war we were all in. There would be nights I stayed on deck looking up at the starry sky, wishing there were a way to escape the world that my father had so carelessly destroyed. I managed to keep a very low profile and if anyone asked who I was, I emphasized my slightly broken British accent and used my mother's middle name. As far as I could tell, no one thought twice.

Our struggles soon turned to danger as we left the Bering Strait and were just about to enter the Eastern Siberian Sea. I'm not going to lie: when we hit the first sheet of ice, I almost had a heart attack. The sound of ice slamming against the bow of the ship echoed in our ears, and soon silence became a foreign concept to us. The other ships attempted to stay in our path, but many met their unfortunate demise with stray sheets of ice. This forced us to stop and rescue as many as we could, but given the frozen temperatures of the water, we couldn't always save everyone.

Two weeks after our departure, we arrived to a rather disappointing sight. A small group of islands stood before us as we docked our massive tanker. Among the crowd I heard the words *Medvezhyi Islands* and *twenty-two miles from*

Ambarchik. I had very little knowledge about Siberia, but I'd taken a few geography electives in college. From what I knew, Ambarchik was an abandoned port city off the coast. But no one had repopulated the area as the harsh winter conditions made the town rather inhospitable.

Thousands of passengers exited their ships and piled into various boats, small enough to maneuver the precarious path between the ice sheets. I expected there would be a commotion of people asking all sorts of questions or just talking amongst themselves, but not a single person even coughed. The sounds of the splashing water and ice scraping against the metal boats increased the growing tension in the air. We awkwardly landed on the beach, where several people stood waiting. Far inland lay the outline of a military base that probably held more people than it appeared to. But the strangest sight, by far, was a four-story metal contraption with three strange protruding pods on the side. In between the pods, in bright yellow letters, read the words BEACON OF HOPE. The length of the structure must have spanned at least six football fields.

It didn't take me long to put the pieces together. There was no cure. The hope these strangers promised was a metal death trap in which to wait out the disaster, however long that would be.

The nervous voyagers began to speak almost all at once, but above the cacophony of voices, I heard people shouting instructions at us as we were being shoved along toward the distant base. Being at the edge of the massive group, I caught glimpses at some of the people in charge. The only thing distinguishing them was the HOPE logo on their large, black coats.

"That is the last ship," I heard a man say in broken English.

"Well, now we have a problem. We have a little over two hundred thousand people to board the *Beacon*. It can't hold that many!" said another, his voice breaking under stress.

I fell behind to gather more information, but my heart nearly jumped out of my chest when the first man said, "I understand the limit, but our whole mission was to rescue as many survivors as possible, Emrys."

I moved closer and awkwardly stood in front of the two men. Their conversation ceased as the man called Emrys turned toward me with a quizzical look. His black scruffy hair, dark blue eyes, and olive skin looked familiar. I just knew that this was my childhood best friend.

"I'm sorry. Civilians must go to the base," started the other man, motioning toward the direction of the location.

Emrys raised a hand, stopping his colleague from continuing. A row of pearly white teeth shined as the corners of his lips turned up. His dark eyes searched mine, and it was like a flood of memories illuminated his face all at once.

"Khyra? Is that really you?" he asked hopefully, stepping closer to me.

All I could do was nod as he wrapped me in a warm, strong hug. "It's been too long!" he exclaimed pulling away from me. "How have you been? No, don't answer that. Come with me—you don't belong among the others."

"Emrys, we don't have the time for tours," exclaimed the man watching Emrys pull me away.

"Dmitriy, this is the woman I've been telling you about. She can help us," said Emrys firmly. I could feel my face scrunch up in confusion. *Me?* How did Emrys know about me?

Dmitriy threw up his hands in defeat and walked away mumbling something in Russian. Emrys guided me toward the metal contraption. "Don't pay him any mind. My cousin has always been paranoid about outsiders knowing the ins and outs of our . . . project."

"I didn't know you had a cousin," I said, surprised. I felt stupid for this being the first thing I said to him after all these years.

Emrys chuckled, possibly reading my mind. "Neither did I until a few years ago."

"Oh," I said, wondering what all I'd missed. "Wait, what did you tell him about me? Did you know I would come? But how could you—what do you know about me, exactly? I mean, we haven't seen each other since we were kids."

Emrys gave me a sideways glance. His eyes gleamed with a knowing look—one he used to give me as children when his abilities allowed him to cheat at games.

"We've heard a great deal about your conflict with your father, Khyra. Your spunk and determination to stop him is why we're all here today. There is much you've missed since we last spoke. Let me catch you up to speed," he said, ushering me into the foreboding metal death trap.

"Wait!" I began, feeling like I missed an important piece of his statement, "You can't give me credit for that! I . . . I didn't really do anything."

He flashed a small grin as he replied, "Ah, but you're forgetting my gift. I have seen all that you've gone through to get here. The court proceedings, the law suits, and the things you have yet to do. You inspired us to create an escape!"

He guided me around the *Beacon*, introducing me to every engineer and scientist we ran into. We passed the living quarters, kitchens, and several dining halls. Circling around toward some higher-end rooms, I noticed there was an indoor garden where some people tended to the plants. Judging by their lab coats, I assumed the group consisted of botanists and possibly a few agriculturists. There were four elevators in total, but we only took two. The upper floors held more quarters and a few recreational sections. This massive structure felt like it would be a good home—that is, if the people were completely fine with not being able to see the light of day again. The few windows we passed allowed for little light to pass through, probably some kind of UV light prevention or something of that nature. I'm sure that I missed a lot during my initial tour of the *Beacon* as Emrys talked quite a lot. In fact, he seemed bubbly and excited, as if he were showing me a new toy.

"And this is probably where you'll be spending most of your time," he said hurriedly, noticing I wasn't really paying close attention.

"Wait, slow down. Emrys, what you've done here is fantastic—I think—at least what I've gathered. I'd love to be part of your team, but I think I'd like to know who else is part of it before I make a decision," I explained as I watched his smile fade away.

For the first time since I'd known him, Emrys grew serious. I could see the gears in his head turning behind his piercing dark eyes. He needed me as more than a citizen. There was something else going on. Without a change in his stoic expression, Emrys suddenly said, "You know what? I'm bored. Let's go on an adventure!"

I had no time to object as he grabbed my hand and we flew down the hallway and out into the freezing cold. Swiftly, he grabbed a team coat off a rack and threw it over my shoulders. I got one arm in as he continued to pull me away from civilization. He spun me into a battery-operated vehicle that reminded me of a golf cart, except instead of wheels, it moved by way of hovering, the four propellers created a small breeze.

Soundlessly, we rose high into the sky, the *Beacon* in its entirety looming below. My eyes widened at the sight as we continued to rise. From the sky, the structure looked like a beetle, with three protruding pods on the outermost parts of each "wing." The front had a massive round window, which I assumed to be another science lab, but the top metal part of the container formed into an arrow with a jagged center. Strange, glowing blue lines connected the inner parts of the arrow, forming a woven pattern that was mesmerizing. Looking back, Emrys intentionally lingered over the *Beacon* so I could get a better view as to what it was. I looked at him as he smiled down on this monstrosity as if it were his most prized possession. Then he shifted the hover vehicle into gear, and we soared over the desolate land until the *Beacon* was no larger than a thumbnail. Emrys stopped the vehicle on the ocean's edge and directed my attention to a beautiful polar bear and her cubs playing on a distant ice shelf. He flipped a few switches and put the vehicle in idle mode. We peacefully hovered, watching what were possibly the last remnants of nature.

"That's . . . beautiful," I stammered. I couldn't remember the last time I'd seen wild animals not struggling to survive.

"They were the first thing I found when I arrived," he reminisced.

My heart hammered in my chest. I had to ask the question that had burned in my mind since our surprise reunion. I gazed at him in awe. "Emrys, what *happened* to you?"

The distant sounds of the wild animals seemed muted in the awkward moment. But the question had to come out, eventually. Absently, he nodded his head and smiled. "Well, it must've started when my best friend was wrongfully taken away from me."

Shortly after my departure, his mother had come down with an unidentified sickness, and passed away. He and his father made do with what they could, but they were both rather miserable without Freya. When Emrys was old enough to go out into the world on his own, he did, in hopes of finding a better living to provide for his father. He was able to send Cornelius letters along with some money, but eventually those came back to Emrys with a stamp on the envelope saying, 'Return to Sender'. Cornelius disappeared without a trace leaving Emrys wondering what became of him.

Just before Crawlis Industries released the second wave of toxins, Emrys was confronted by his mysterious estranged cousin in a bar just outside of London. The organization Dmitriy worked for had been keeping an eye on Emrys behind the scenes, and sent him to recruit Emrys to their cause of saving humanity. Several private companies from around the world had donated the materials used to build the *Beacon*. These specific companies had foreseen possible disasters pertaining to my father's operation, since the original sickness began when I was a child. Individuals like Dmitriy's father worked with one of these companies in order to create innovative materials to be used for technology almost identical to that used in the *Beacon*.

Dmitriy carried on after his father passed, and practically designed the *Beacon* himself. At this point in his story, Emrys revealed to me that Dmitriy had a special power: that of invention. According to legend, Dragos Bates, the cousins' grandfather, had crossed a coven of witches when he'd killed the brother of a high priestess. As the story went, Dragos had made a deal with a warlock—whom he personally knew—to find a magical cure to heal Dragos's sister. She had an illness that medicine of that time could not cure. The warlock did everything he could to heal the woman, but she just got worse. Eventually, she passed away. Grief-stricken, Dragos killed the warlock, and an entire coven came raining down on him. The high priestess cast a powerful curse of servitude on Dragos and his lineage. One of Drago's children was forced to see the future, the other was afflicted with knowledge above human comprehension. This would continue to spread throughout the generations and at times make social lives difficult for the family. Emrys's father was a psychic, Dmitriy's dad an incredible inventor. Emrys's own vision had played a vital role in the construction of the *Beacon*. Each and every flash of an image acted as a specific deadline for when parts were to be completed. Recently, the visions had ended, leaving everyone in a frenzy trying to prevent future disasters.

But the Toxin—the event that had led to mankind's ruin—was one Emrys could not prevent, despite what he envisioned.

"Emrys, I'm so sorry . . ." I began as his story ended.

"Please don't blame yourself. My life has never been easy. It's been an adventure, and one I wouldn't trade for anything at that! After all, it led me back to you, didn't it?" he replied optimistically.

"So, do I *want* to know how I fit in all this?" I asked nervously.

Emrys closed his eyes, as if he'd dreaded this moment. His voice was hesitant. "We need a scientist who can identify general toxins in the atmosphere. You're the last person alive who can do so."

"The Toxin isn't going to leave our atmosphere anytime soon," I replied, casting my eyes down to my hands in my lap. I'd wrestled with this fact constantly, and it never seemed to get easier to accept.

"No, but *we* are," he said with a hopeful smile, reaching down to take one of my hands in his. "The *Beacon* will transport us through the galaxy in search of a new home. We need you to help us find a suitable planet."

"A suitable planet?" I repeated slowly. "You're telling me that that massive metal . . . *thing* is a . . . a spaceship?

Are you insane?" I almost couldn't believe what he was saying. It had never been proven that life anywhere other than on Earth was sustainable.

"It's our only option at the moment, Khyra. Believe me, we've exhausted all other ideas of how to save humanity. But even you have to admit that staying here will destroy us all eventually," said Emrys.

I sat back in my seat and shook my head in disbelief. "Emrys, spaceships are incredibly difficult to build, let alone one that can carry thousands of people. We're on Earth, not some science fiction based planet! It can't be done!"

"Magic, not science fiction." His mouth quirked with a small smile of pride.

I was shocked by his comment and stared at him until he continued. "My family has magic of sorts, as I explained. Dmitriy constructed half that ship, and most of it was created through ideas of his own. Therefore, it's magic that made the *Beacon* possible. So, the correct term you're looking for is fantasy, not science fiction."

I gave up arguing with him. After everything I'd gone through since that point, I still didn't fully understand this sort of magic. I didn't even believe in it. But here I was, hovering in an aircraft next to my childhood friend who'd predicted where and when I would show up back in his life and recognized me after all these years.

I ended up changing the topic as we hovered back toward the base. "I admire your optimism, Emrys. But if you hadn't noticed, I'm not well liked among the scientific community—or any community for that matter . . . due to what? Oh yeah, that's right: my father basically ended the world."

He shook his head in protest, then grabbed my chin, turning my face to his. "You are not your father. Besides, I've made certain that your father's transgressions against the world are not placed on you."

Every warning signal went off in my head. I'd observed humanity long enough to know Emrys was wrong. The rest of my family was dead, so the next best thing was to focus the blame on the one remaining member.

But no matter how much I protested he refused to listen. Instead, he babbled on about how helpful I'd be while dragging me back into the *Beacon* and to the room he'd initially wanted to show me. He smoothly blocked the door before we entered and said, "All I ask is that you give this a chance. I promise, if you decide to have no part in this, you can join the ranks of the other regular citizens."

I looked into his pleading eyes and sighed in defeat. "All right; you've got a deal."

"Wonderful!" He opened the door. "Let me introduce you to the New Earth Expedition Team!"

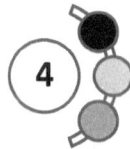

4

At first glance, the room was full of computers. Some lined the walls with glowing panels, while a holographic map of the Milky Way hovered in the center of the room, with several people in a deep conversation surrounding it. As I looked beyond the tech, the room curved into an enormous window with a perfect view of the ocean.

"Everyone, I'd like to introduce you to Khyra Crawford. She has agreed to help us find a new home," said Emrys, motioning to me in a professional tone.

For a moment, the room fell silent. I could hear the quiet beeps of the computers. All eyes were on me and I felt like a sideshow, one that the crowd silently detested behind their fake smiles. Then, someone finally spoke up out of nowhere to say what was likely on everyone's mind: "I thought you were joking when you said she was the last scientist left. What a shame." The speaker was a short, college-aged guy—a thick lock of brown hair draped down his forehead as he glanced up from his tablet.

"Dr. Colbert, that'll be enough. Without Khyra's help, all of humanity will be lost," Emrys said, defending me.

"If she's anything like her old man, we might be better off," spat the kid.

I don't know what came over me. I owed these strangers no excuse, and I didn't even want to be part of the team, but I couldn't let that snide comment slide.

"Look, you know, it's because of my old man that I *became* an environmentalist. And you know what I got for my decision? He disowned me. I left home at sixteen and had to work from the ground up for my degree. I never saw my family again. Check your facts before you start throwing accusations," I said with all the spite I could muster. I almost forgot other people were in the room until someone began applauding me.

"That was spectacularly said, cousin," came a prestigious male voice from out of nowhere.

My heart sank when my cousin, John Oak, stepped out of the group. To be honest, of all my family, I wished he was among the dead the most. It was just my luck that I had to see his arrogant, selfish face again.

"I am *so* glad to see you're alive and well, Khyra!" He pompously strolled my way to give me a hug.

"Likewise," I struggled to say, glaring at Emrys from over John's shoulder. I didn't have to be psychic to know that he dreaded our next conversation.

John pulled away and put an arm around me as if we were close friends. "Well, Dr. Andrew Colbert has already introduced himself. He holds three science degrees, despite his young age. However, his expertise on our voyage falls more toward the worlds of astrophysics and astronomy. Oh, and I'm certain Emrys has already told you about his cousin Dmitriy's role." He looked toward Emrys's cousin's direction.

Dmitriy's countenance was a little different than Emrys's, but his demeanor and appearance were similar. Same straight black hair, penetrating dark eyes, but he had this air of nerdiness about him. Don't get me wrong—most of my friends were tech nerds in college—but Dmitriy wasn't your average, stereotypical nerd. He appeared very fit, around six feet. Quite the ladies' man. But by his shy apprehension, he seemed too modest for that.

"Now that gentleman over there"—John nodded toward a tall man leaning down toward someone in a lab coat, motioning to a series of what appeared to be constellations displayed across the screen. His blond crew cut made him appear military-like, but his demeanor held a more professional air to it than the usual upstanding soldier type—"Lukas Grunewald is the Chancellor of Germany; or rather, he was. Anyway, his knowledge of working with the citizens of his country has allowed this operation to run smoothly and effectively. Remember when I was enrolled in the Royal Navy a while back?" I slowly nodded, signaling him to continue.

"I was promoted as Marshal of the Royal Navy right before the outbreak. I met Lukas over there while stationed in Hamburg and, well, I'd say we've made quite a team, working to keep as many people alive as we can, both then and since."

Whether John had helped thousands of people, it still didn't excuse his past sins as a child. I may have forgiven, but had not forgotten, regardless of being united with Emrys years later.

"That's very brave of you," I finally replied, my tone not entirely sincere.

Ignoring the tension permeating the air, John uncomfortably replied, "Yes, well, we all must do our part."

My eyes moved back to Lukas and as I studied him, I realized I'd seen him on television. Before the end of the world, that was.

He'd come across as a quiet individual who only spoke up when needed. During those times, he was breaking up arguments. Rumors had swirled when he was nominated chancellor. The rumors increased when he actually won the seat; stories of his past were blown up all over major worldwide news headlines. Word had it his great-great-grandfather was a high-ranking soldier in the Nazi regime back in World War II. Even so, Lukas had taken his position seriously, and had fought to take care of Germany and those around him.

"But enough small talk: it's time for you to familiarize yourself with the technology we have," said John, interrupting the awkward silence. "We'll leave you and Emrys to it then."

Lukas and John then proceeded to exit the room, followed by Colbert. The door slid closed behind them. I returned to glaring at Emrys, who winced in anticipation of what I was going to say.

"You lied to me. You didn't tell me John was involved in this operation. Of all people, Emrys!" My words bounced off the metal walls, covering the noises of the computers.

"No, I just didn't tell you everything," said Emrys, lifting his hands in defense. He knew exactly where this was going and because he was psychic, I had no chance of winning the ensuing argument.

My disgruntled silence prompted him to continue. "Look, I'm not asking you to become friends, let alone forgive him, Khyra. What he did to us—to you—was wrong. But please consider this: our world is dying, and humanity is on the verge of extinction. I think it'd be unwise to allow childhood feuds dictate the future of our existence, don't you? We were kids, it happened, time to grow up."

My mouth shut with a snap. How could I argue with a well-rehearsed statement like that? All I could do was give him a disapproving look, wishing I could make a biting comeback statement.

"Not that I don't appreciate this conversation, but I believe we should get to work," Dmitriy chimed in right behind me. I jumped at his voice, realizing we weren't alone.

"Come. I'd like to show you some of our findings on the Toxin," said Dmitriy kindly, exchanging a quick glance with his cousin. He lightly placed his hand on my shoulder and guided me to an adjacent conference room set up with a presentation. I took a seat at the head of the table and focused my attention on Dmitriy.

According to the *Beacon* team's research, the people at the Siberian base were the last of humanity. But most of these people were immune to the Toxin. Emrys was the first to discover this anomaly. Of the horrible deeds my father had committed, he accidentally did one thing right. Silisk, the forgotten cure for the first round of toxins, had granted its hosts immunity to the second outbreak of lethal pollutants. Unfortunately, there was no way of knowing if our offspring would have the same reaction. We could only hope that we didn't stay long enough to find out.

Over the next few weeks, I learned everything I could in their database about the Toxin. But the rest I would have to discover on my own through observation and experimentation. What little I gleaned from the EWFA helped some, but I had very little pure samples to compare the research to. Aside from testing and observing day and night, I spent most of my time alone but occasionally socialized with Emrys and Dmitriy. As for my cousin? I avoided him at all costs. Not that it was difficult; he mostly spent his time debating with Lukas on when we should leave Earth.

From what I understood, they expected the ship to be completely ready in a year . . . but the Toxin had other plans. Temperatures began to rise due to the sudden climate change the Toxin triggered. This made the Arctic Ocean swimmable. At first, it was nice to watch people enjoy the change, as it brought back a sense of normalcy. But this was wrong—very wrong—and I had to find out if we were in the midst of another disaster.

All the computer models showed me nothing I didn't already know. But one morning, after a pot of coffee and several power naps, I had a new idea. One of the models gave an overview of the ozone layer, including the depleted areas. Nothing much had changed from what I already knew, except for a few random holes, but nothing like the ozone hole over Antarctica. No, these were much smaller and nowhere in proximity to each other. One of these holes happened to appear above where Emrys had introduced me to the polar bears. Out of morbid curiosity, I decided to check on them again, borrowing a hovercraft to do so. But I couldn't make it within half a mile of the bears. My skin began to burn from a strange heat emanating from that direction. Nervously, I pulled out a pair of high-tech binoculars that I'd borrowed from Dmitriy, and nearly lost my lunch. The land was scorched, and any ice that once floated in the water had long since melted away. All that remained of the poor polar bear family were dried up carcasses. Their fur covered the now-blackened, visible soil, and small pieces of skin that clung to their bones bubbled in the invisible, searing heat. This wasn't just an ozone hole; the dangerous effects of the sun and the foreign toxic air had created an entirely new monster. This was the future, and there was no way of knowing when *we'd* be next.

I sped back so fast I thought the vehicle gained a gearshift. No one seemed to notice my hasty arrival, but I received a number of curious looks as I tumbled out of the hover vessel trying to run inside the *Beacon*. I vaguely remembered a scheduled meeting on the bridge, and all I could hope was that the team would still be there. My legs felt like jelly as I raced down the halls, my pounding heart masking the metallic sounds my feet made with each step.

I fumbled with the switch on the door before it slid open and I fell into the room. After regaining my composure, I faced the team. Whatever conversation I interrupted seemed insignificant to them now.

"We have a big problem," I said.

"I would say so," said Colbert, stunned. "You broke the door."

I looked behind me to see the door sliding open and closed repeatedly. I rolled my eyes, mentally scolding myself for ruining even more credibility. Already I could see this conversation going horribly wrong. Returning my attention to the team, all but Emrys seemed to find the situation humorous. But my friend was the only one to see the horror still etched on my face.

"Khyra, you don't look well. What's wrong?" he asked, trying to refocus the conversation.

I couldn't tell them we needed to leave immediately. They'd just brush everything I'd say aside. This conversation had to be calculated. Ignoring the suspicious glares in the room, I turned my attention to the cousins.

"Dmitriy, how much longer before we can set off?"

Like Emrys, Dmitriy noticed something off, and with furrowed brows replied, "We're on schedule to leave in December."

"Two months," I said, mostly to myself. "We can't leave any sooner?"

"That'd be too risky, Khyra," said Emrys with a strange look. I knew that expression anywhere. He had seen something—something he'd rather not say.

"Risky or not, we have to act fast. The ozone layer is depleting at a much faster rate than usual," I replied, ignoring his hidden meaning and bracing myself for controversy.

"So? We'll just import sunblock. That's not exactly a deadly situation," said Colbert sarcastically.

"I'd agree with you—that is, if we weren't dealing with a deadly poison that can morph into whatever it wants," I replied honestly. When I received expressions of disbelief and confusion, I continued. "Think of it like this: a magnifying glass and sunlight are not dangerous alone, but together they can start a fire. I've personally seen the effects of this very scenario occurring with the lack of ozone layer and the Toxin. Small holes have been popping up on our radars, but they've seemed to be random. We don't know what the Toxin is made of, nor do we have the time to figure it out—we haven't been able to so far, and we've been working on that very question since the outbreak began. We're out of time. If we don't leave now, we are all certainly going to die."

"My scans would have alerted me if the ozone was that close to being destroyed," said Colbert frantically searching his tablet, "I don't believe its depleting at the rate you claim. With all the technology that we have, it'd be impossible to miss! It's . . . it's unheard of!" Colbert pointed out.

"So is a toxin that can eradicate the human race, yet here we are," said Grunewald. He'd never spoken to me before, let alone publicly defended me.

"Well, where's your proof?" Colbert asked. No matter what I did, how hard I worked, or what evidence I gathered, he always seemed desperate to prove me wrong.

"Drive fifteen miles northeast of here and you'll run into the boiling carcasses of a polar bear family. That is, if you don't burn up yourself within a half mile of the location," I spat, holding up my reddened hand. "Look, I'm being serious: the small holes in the ozone have been coming with no warning. It's as bad as playing Russian roulette."

"Actually, it's worse," said Dmitriy, who silently moved toward the computers. "Judging by these radars, Russian roulette would be safer. Khyra is correct—we must leave now."

Colbert opened his mouth to protest, but whatever snarky comment he had was drowned out by the horrendous screams of thousands of people. We all bolted out of the room and ran down the hall. I took the lead. From behind me, I heard John yell to someone to start the engines. For a moment, it felt good that he believed in me, but when we reached outside under the overhang of the entrance, the feeling vanished. Thousands of people shoved past us, trying to get inside the ship. But many more were already dead from the new monster that the sun and Toxin created. The worst sight of all was the others running from the distant base, their silhouettes collapsing from the torture of being steamed alive. Fortunately, there were still a couple thousand near the ship that could be saved, though they floundered as their skin began to blister.

"There's nothing we can do for the rest—let's set off now!" John yelled above the noise.

How he'd become a leader in a militaristic position was beyond me. He sounded like the coward I'd always known. That's when I knew I needed to do something. John held me back and said, "I won't let you die!"

I whipped around and slapped him. "You're such a coward, always burying your head in the sand! I'll help save whomever I can, even if it scars your precious ego! The military didn't change you. You *never* changed. If you won't help save those people, then get out of my way!"

No words were exchanged among the team members as I bolted toward a massive tarp, ignoring the searing pain of the blistering sun on my bare flesh. I was prepared to carry out my plan alone, but Emrys and Dmitriy came up alongside me, grabbing the other corners of the tarp. No words, just expressions that told me they were following my lead. I jumped into the nearest vehicle while the other two found their own.

I winced as the chemically laced atmosphere burned my hands as I pulled the tarp over my head. Glancing at the others, I saw they were scrambling to protect themselves in the same situation. Covering every part of our bodies, we created an umbrella for those still struggling. I don't know how many we protected, but our primary concern was to hold it there for as long as we could. But it didn't take long before even the exposed parts of our vehicles began melting. With heavy hearts, we returned to the *Beacon*, rumbling in preparation for takeoff. All three of us dropped the tarp and one by one dove into the ship, leaving our vehicles to melt. The door closed behind us as the stench of burned flesh stung our noses. We climbed over bodies, some of which we weren't sure were alive. But from the looks of things, we saved thousands more than anticipated; apparently many had already been nearby when the ozone layer fell. Emrys congratulated me on how well my idea had worked. But the truth was, I'd just been guessing.

Emrys and Dmitriy continued following me down the hall, both asking what I was planning to do next. I had all intentions of yelling at my cousin, but it wasn't easy finding him or even maneuvering through the thousands of new arrivals. The ship began to take off, but with incredible difficulty due to the unexpected departure. At first, I grew concerned we would be stuck on Earth, in a metal ship that would slowly cook us like an oversized oven. But when I finally found John, he and the other team members were staring out a side window. I could see the horror etched on their faces. I came up beside Colbert and looked outside to see the *Beacon* had brought us into space with ease, and we were relatively safe. But I wish I could've said the same for our home world. Earth was covered in a sickly green film. The Toxin alone was invisible, but the sun's effect added a color that matched its deadliness.

Anger boiled up within me. I was tired of being ignored and blamed for my father's crimes. I was my own person, and it was time I proved it. I tore my attention away from the terrible sight and looked at Colbert, who despite the terror on his face, refused to look at me.

"Is this proof enough?"

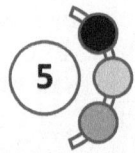

5

As we soared off into the starry unknown, we ran into a few minor glitches here and there along our way. At least, I gathered that much from the engineers that occasionally ran around attending to their specific jobs. But I never got a straight answer out of them as to what was going on. I rarely spoke to the team, including Emrys. The drama that the group as a whole had inflicted upon themselves was more than I could handle. Besides, the civilians were in desperate need of help and comfort—something only a young nurse and I saw as important.

We met under unusual circumstances. A technical malfunction occurred in a part of the spaceship, which resulted in several people injuring themselves, myself included. It wasn't anything huge, just a few minor cuts and bruises. But the biggest injury of all was the egos of the crew members. They started casting blame onto each other. I walked away from the arguing and headed toward the infirmary. I had only been there once, to help the people injured before our departure, but hadn't met whoever ran it. The infirmary consisted of a large open room with limited beds. Those were only used for the truly ill or injured. But due to its size, I found it to be the only place of quiet.

As I opened the door to my moment of solitude, I was greeted with a rather perturbed, "I'll be with you in a second."

"It's fine, please take your time!" I replied, taken aback by such a coarse response.

A pretty nurse emerged from behind a closed certain. Her black, curly hair was tied back in a large hair tie, several strands escaping their hold. She stood a little over five feet, and her chestnut skin was flawless. All her other features were covered by a lab coat. She came across as a woman who was not to be trifled with. She rolled her dark brown eyes at the pitiful moaning coming from behind. "Ryan, you're fine!

It's just a sprain! If you'd stop arm wrestling people, maybe this wouldn't happen!"

"Alice, I'm bored!" exclaimed a young man, following after her.

The nurse whirled around. "Tough! We're all bored here. Now go find someone else to bother!"

The disgruntled man stormed out of the infirmary muttering a slew of colorful words. Alice looked at me exasperatedly. "Don't tell me you've been arm wrestling, too."

"No, just a few cuts and bruises. There was a malfunction down the hall. The crew was arguing . . . I . . . I was just looking for some peace," I replied, afraid I was going to get yelled at.

She crossed her arms. "You're not going to find that here, miss. There hasn't been peace in this room since we started. Every day I'm taking in more and more burn victims. I can't stand the likes of guys like Ryan, who only come here because they've got nothing better to do."

"Well, I'm here and I've got plenty of better things to do," I said, hoping to lighten the mood.

It worked. Alice smirked at my remark and nodded. "Let me see those cuts and bruises."

At first it was small talk, but then our conversation grew deeper.

"Got three kids, single mom, living in Chicago. Or at least that's what my life was like on Earth. Now I'm a single mom of three in space," said Alice morbidly as she sewed up a particularly deep cut.

Stupidly, I impulsively asked, "What happened to their father? Was he killed by the Toxin?"

Alice tugged a bit harshly on the thread as she tied it off. "Dunno. He hasn't been in the kids' life for . . . a long time. I haven't seen him since the outbreak started, so I'm gonna assume that's the case."

"Alice, I'm sorry. I honestly didn't mean to pry," I apologized. The last thing I needed was to make enemies—after all, the spaceship was only so big.

The young nurse stared at me for the longest time, confused by my reaction. Then she replied, "You mean, you didn't hear the rumors?"

Just as I was about to ask what she meant, a horde of injured came in. A young woman led the crowd. "Nurse White? Nurse White! Please help—these are burn victims that were forgotten in the chaos of the departure!"

"How—? Ugh, never mind. Khyra, you're my assistant today! Get me those syringes and grab loads of towels!" she ordered me.

And that's how my friendship with Alice White began. She never told me what her vague response meant, but many of the people on the ship had things to say. Rumors swarmed that her children's father was a drug dealer of sorts. I heard people mentioning he was all over the news before Earth fell. Of course, I never paid attention to things like that, I had far bigger things to worry about. Now, whether what the rumors and media said was true or not I never asked Alice. Her indifference about his well being told me enough. Unlike most of the people on the ship, I didn't hold that against her. She was the most kindhearted and hardworking person I had ever met. It was a privilege to work alongside her.

We treated all the burn victims and were surprised to find some celebrities who had managed to escape the confines of their Hollywood homes, somehow finding their way north, and eventually onto the ship. Some of them even joined forces with us to find suitable living space for the others. After the initial chaos of our departure, we discovered that there were more people than living quarters.

Once we doubled up on space within the rooms, those remaining found the dining hall and rec room to be comfortable places to sleep. Between Alice, several celebrities, and myself, we divided up the responsibilities of taking care of the health of the passengers. Alice wanted to conduct more research on the immune and non-immune, and I offered to assist. The celebrities offered to act as liaisons between the passengers and expedition team. And that's where they got their name, the Liaisons—to this day, there are several people on Diraetus who are directly related to these wonderful leaders . . . some even following in their ancestors' paths, becoming actors . . . but I'm getting ahead of myself. Our plans for a coexistent space society seemed ideal, but due to the confined space and cultural differences, so many fights erupted.

Sometimes, the Liaisons could defuse the situation, but a few times Emrys and Dmitriy got involved. That's when the initial *Beacon* development team discovered what we had been doing. They'd locked themselves away on the bridge for so long it was like we had two separate countries within one ship. The team began extending their duties to include checking on us. It was mostly Emrys who would discreetly observe from a distance, trying not to interfere. I'd like to think he was impressed with how well we did, but I just think he missed talking to me.

But truthfully, I was enjoying my time with Alice. Having another woman in my life somehow balanced out the insane testosterone levels I had to deal with from the main members of the team. I remember one particular time where she and I were in the infirmary. It was the only time I can recall when no patients were occupying it! She was going over samples of the Toxin and comparing it to other diseases on her computer.

"I don't understand," I admitted. "I thought you were a nurse."

"Technically," Alice said, her eyes glued to the screen, "but before the world ended, I was trying to get my doctorate. Honestly, it was my passion to get into pediatrics."

I flashed a smile. That was a career I could see my friend pursuing. Wanting to know more about her discoveries, I asked, "Have you found anything unusual about the Toxin? Could there be an antidote?"

Alice leaned back in her seat with a sigh. She stared down at the Toxin sample that sat under a microscope. Her brows furrowed, as if waiting for the disease to magically give her an answer. Then she shook her head. "I've spent hours researching this. And I've only been able to find out more about what it is. Nothing about how to prevent or stop it."

"But that's a good thing—learning more about what it *is* can help us develop ways to combat it!"

She gave me an exhausted smile. "That's just it, though. The Toxin is a little bit of every disease we've ever encountered."

"But it's manmade! How is that even possible?" I asked, looking at her screens for proof of her claims.

"Khyra, I gotta ask—did you know what types of chemicals your dad used in his facilities?" she looked at me, concerned.

"I . . . no, no I don't. When I defied the family and struck out on my own, I lost all access to the information that likely could've helped us the most," I replied guiltily.

"Don't worry about it now. It's in the past," Alice assured me. "If it's any consolation, there *is* one upside to all of this."

"The Toxin that wiped out most of the human race has an upside to it? Oh, this is going to be good," I said sarcastically.

Alice smiled and rolled her eyes at my snarky comment, but then turned to her data. "Yes. You see, I've been trying to observe what would happen over time with the Toxin. I have no idea how, but it's managed to become part of our DNA. Some, like you, are immune, but that doesn't mean your children will be. It's powerful, I'll admit that much, but its life expectancy isn't. I'd say, give it a couple generations, and those who get the Toxin might have only flu-like symptoms."

"There's still hope for the human race!" I said, relieved.

Sadly, I'd spoken too soon. A young woman tumbled into the infirmary in hysterics. She clutched her stomach in obvious pain and could barely stand. Simultaneously, Alice and I rushed to her side. Alice immediately asked the woman a series of questions. "Ultrasound" was about the only thing I understood. The poor woman was pregnant—*was* being the key word. I assisted Alice every way I could, although most of that consisted of calming the woman down. After Alice did all she could for the woman, she gave her something to make her relax enough to fall asleep.

"She's the fifth woman to come to me since our departure. It makes sense, really. The Toxin affects every part of us. My first priority is to find a resolution for this reproduction issue," said Alice quietly.

"But won't it take longer to understand the Toxin and its behavior?" I asked, trying to understand her priorities.

Alice looked at me with such sadness in her eyes and said, in a tone so broken that I nearly cried, "Khyra, if I don't fix this reproduction issue, we won't have to worry about the next generation getting the Toxin."

Alice tried finding formulas that would limit or suppress the effects of the Toxin, or at the very least allow reproduction. And she eventually did, but that wasn't until we'd almost reached the Chronosalis Galaxy nearly a decade later. Even a thousand years later, though, people still become afflicted with the Toxin. Fortunately, it isn't widespread, and, as Alice had predicted, its symptoms were similar to the flu. And over the years of genetics and mutations, some people have managed to survive the Toxin and get better on their own.

Through Alice's endless days of research, I did everything she asked of me. But my services were soon required elsewhere. I was in the dining hall, enjoying my coffee and solitude, when I saw Emrys approaching from the corner of my eye. I hadn't seen him in weeks, so I was surprised by his serious facial expression.

"This can't be good. Eyebrows scrunched and shoulders bunched up? Okay, spill!" I said with a sly smile.

"You know me too well, so I'll just cut to the chase. I could use your help with deciphering something."

I looked at him suspiciously. "Okay, Mr. Cryptic, what is it?"

"It's on the bridge, if you'll come with me," he replied hesitantly, shuffling from one foot to the other. I gave him a smile and rose to follow him, throwing away the remains of my trash in a compost bin which would be later used as fertilizer for the gardens.

This sounded much more than a simple deciphering problem. I swallowed the last bit of my coffee, now wishing it was something stronger. "I guess Alice can manage without me for a while."

The look of relief on his face was priceless. He looked as excited as when he'd first introduced me to the *Beacon*. I tried to keep up with his fast pace, but when we reached the bridge, I had to catch my breath. Dmitriy was already there, tablet in hand, waiting for our arrival.

"I told you she'd come," Dmitriy chuckled, flashing Emrys a knowing look.

Ignoring the chuckling, I sighed. "Okay, I'm here: What do you want to show me?"

"This," Colbert called from behind a computer module set in the middle of the room. He pressed a couple buttons, bringing up the holographic map that now displayed an outline of a planet.

"We're currently hovering over this planet and we think it'll work as a home, but we wanted your expert opinion."

I inched toward the map and examined the properties of the planet, all eyes on me. After fidgeting with the dials on the main panel, a huge screen appeared along with the planet. At first, I was repulsed by the colors. It looked like a big, neon green ball. Not something I would personally find inviting. I read the properties displayed next to the planet. The breathability was thin. It'd be like living on top of Mount Everest, to say nothing of the planet's surface itself. Venus would be cooler in comparison! Our only means of surviving, provided the atmosphere and heat didn't kill us first, would be to live underground. Biting back every snarky comment, I shook my head. "I'm sorry, but this planet's atmosphere doesn't have enough oxygen, and the summer months would burn us alive. But for your first attempt, it was a pretty good shot."

"Actually, it's our fifth planet," said Colbert sheepishly, his face flushed rosy pink.

"Wait, fifth? We can't have been in space for that long . . . have we?" I asked, annoyed that they just now asked for my help.

"We've been in space for three years. You'd know that if you were up here, doing what we asked you to do, instead of playing hero," said John acidly.

I was very surprised at the length of our voyage. But being in space and preoccupied tends to distract one from crossing off the days. "Well, someone had to play hero for those people. After all, saving humanity is the point of this mission—or in all your bickering, did you forget that?" I shot back.

"And we're grateful to you and the other leaders of the civilians. You've saved many lives," interrupted Grunewald.

Following the chancellor's lead, I changed the topic. "So how are you finding these planets?"

"Through an incomplete algorithm," said Dmitriy, looking ashamed. "Like the majority of this ship, we didn't have the chance to complete it before our hasty departure. In theory, it was supposed to allow the *Beacon* to carry us through space at warp speed and drop out when we neared planets that the late astronomers believed were habitable. Now, we travel at warp speed, but when we drop out, there's no telling what type of planet we'll come across. We're farther out in space than even the conspiracy theorists imagined."

"How far, exactly?" I asked, not sure I wanted to know the answer.

"We passed the Perseus Arm six months ago," said Colbert, wincing at my horrified expression. "And there's no telling when we'll reach the end of the galaxy."

"This isn't possible!" I cried, collapsing into a chair from shock, trying to wrap my head around the idea that we were sitting at the edge of the known galaxy.

Colbert chuckled and replied, "Neither is a man-made chemical that can boil people alive, sweetheart."

I quirked a smile at that. Maybe Colbert actually grew up some since we last spoke. I guess tragedies and near-death experiences could do that to a person.

"Dmitriy, is there any way you can complete the algorithm?" I asked, hoping they were doing more than winging it.

"Not without causing severe damage to the other software systems. Our best chance of survival is trying to find a pattern in the jumps and maybe, just maybe, we can manipulate it somehow."

"Well, now that we're all caught up, there's no time to waste! Let's get to work," John said, a bit too cheerfully.

I wish I could say things got better from that conversation, but it didn't.

Colbert was not as sarcastic, but his growing paranoia was no better substitute. Dmitriy holed himself up on the bridge; his attempts at reconfiguring the algorithm seemed endless. John was civil toward me unless no one was around—then our arguing continued. Fortunately, Grunewald seemed to always be nearby, ready to step in if he needed. I think he understood that I didn't want to fight with John. It was always nice to have someone ready to fight in my corner. For their efforts of keeping the peace among the citizens, the Liaisons became honorary members of the team and they were all very welcomed. But when word got out how much trouble we were in, the Liaisons weren't happy with the secrecy.

While nearly all of humanity was in a frenzy, Emrys and I found comfort in each other's company. At first, he would simply share my workload between the bridge and helping Alice. Then we somehow gradually shifted to spending time alone, whether it was talking over coffee or finding an area away from curious gazes. There were even nights, in between jumps, that we would find a window, secluded from the rest of the people, and just gaze at the stars. It was as if we picked up our childhood friendship from what felt like a lifetime ago, and it blossomed into something neither of us expected.

Love. I know it sounds cliché, but so what? I'd never felt love of any kind from anyone else before, except for my mother and Daniel, but that wasn't until much later in my life. This . . . *this* love came from the moment we met—it was something that blossomed into a romance that not even the great authors of Earth could imagine. Our love for each other grew along with our trust. I didn't care that he could read my mind with his abilities, I had nothing to hide and neither did he. I guess that's the best way to explain the next phase of our lives.

A few months later, a strand of the flu virus made its way through the ship—thankfully, not the Toxin. This wasn't abnormal; it occurred every once and a while. It became a problem for Alice, as it was a challenge to differentiate between the two illnesses. And although I'd been safe from the flu before, this time I caught the bug too. But my symptoms differed slightly from the rest. Others had a cough, sore throat, fever, and headache, but not me. Alice informed me none of those affected had the same symptoms, which, to her frustration, made the illness itself harder to treat.

I avoided going to her if I could help it. But, sometimes the vertigo accompanied with the nausea made completing my duties almost impossible. Emrys and even Dmitriy acted strangely around me, as if I was going to drop at any second. Sometimes I even saw them conversing in secret, their whispered conversations seeming panicked.

For a while, I was able to brush it off as two people who just cared about me. But that's when the hallucinations began. I'd hoped they were due to a spike in my temperature, but I had no fever. And the images I saw in these hallucinations were constant, which from what I knew didn't match any illness. I would first see flashing lights, then a beautiful planet similar to Earth's size, but its appearance was surreal. Fluffy pink clouds covered much of the globe, and areas where water could be seen appeared turquoise in color. As for the land? It consisted of various shades of green, with specks of chocolate brown. From a distance, I'd say the planet was just a big ball of cotton candy. Sometimes in the visions I'd see smaller ships leaving the *Beacon* to go to the planet, but almost always, I'd see the *Beacon* itself getting sucked into a wormhole of some kind.

The images would hit me at random, and they'd send a shooting pain through my head. Eventually, I learned to cope with it, and was able to hide the pain in front of people. Until one day where it all came crashing down.

I stumbled down the hall, trying to conceal the intense vertigo that began altering my vision. I was heading toward the bridge for a team meeting and already I was running late. This was the third time my illness had made me late for a meeting and it was only a matter of time before it was no longer a viable excuse to John.

When I slid into the bridge, the meeting had just begun. My near-tardy arrival didn't cause too much commotion but by this time, I didn't care. Sweat dripped down my face, and my racing heart echoed in my ears. To this day I can't recall what that meeting was about, as a full vision redirected my attention—one where all the images of my hallucinations finally merged together as if they were telling a story.

The map revealed another planet—one that could support human life—but the team was in disagreement. Colbert seemed scared and desperate to call this planet home, and it wasn't until I looked out the massive window that I understood why. Ahead of us lay some kind of glowing wormhole full of swirling iridescent colors and stars. It should've been sucking us in, but we remained stationary. That's when I realized this wasn't a wormhole, but rather a portal. I didn't know *where* we were in the galaxy at this point, but I understood Colbert's panic. The portal was the only direction we could go.

Colbert and thousands of other people left for the foreign planet in the next vision. In addition to the remainder of the civilians, all that remained were half of the Liaisons, and the rest of the *Beacon* management team. Alice was among those who'd decided to stay behind. I watched myself push a few buttons and press the *Beacon* forward and away from the people we were forever leaving behind. The portal created such a horrific strobe effect we all collapsed to the ground, shielding our eyes from the powerful lights.

"Khyra, Khyra, darling, please wake up!" came Emrys's pleading voice.

My eyes flickered open and my once-blurred vision now became clear. I must've fallen during my episode, as Emrys held me in his arms, staring down at me. His face was a combination of terror and excitement.

"I saw . . . I saw . . ." I stuttered groggily.

Emrys wiped away a few stray tears from my cheek and calmly replied, "What did you see?"

"The future," I replied, knowing I'd be scoffed at, though not by my psychic friend.

"I figured as much," he said, not the least surprised.

"Emrys, what's going on?" I heard myself ask, although I felt quite distant from my body.

He looked up at who I presumed was Dmitriy. My body felt far too heavy to move, let alone turn my head. Emrys silently nodded and looked back at me: "You're pregnant."

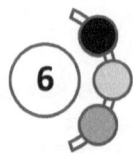

6

Pregnant. I don't know if I even uttered a sound at his comment. I felt so weak I passed out, and it was some time before I regained consciousness. But even returning to a semiconscious state wasn't easy. My hearing came to me before my other senses, and I heard the strangest conversation between Alice, Emrys, and Dmitriy.

"I have three little boys and am also a certified nurse. I think I know a thing or two about pregnancy. Now let me do my job!" exclaimed Alice, who sounded rather insulted.

"We understand, Ms. White," said Dmitriy carefully, "but the child Khyra is carrying isn't ordinary."

"Yeah, yeah, I heard the story. Cursed family, magic babies . . . but regardless of the child's potential abilities, it *is* still a baby, and Khyra is still about to become a new mother. She needs guidance and proper health care."

"And I appreciate that. What we're trying to explain is that this pregnancy will be unlike any that you've seen or experienced," said Emrys.

"What do you mean?" I mumbled, struggling to sit up. I expected to be in the infirmary, but I was instead inside Emrys's quarters—one of the few rooms that had only one person living in it. The trio was at the door and when I announced I was conscious, Emrys hastily came to my side and sat on the edge of the bed.

"How are you feeling?" he asked, avoiding the elephant in the room.

"I'm feeling much better . . . and not at all pregnant," I replied, waiting for an explanation.

"You wouldn't notice—it's all part of the curse," said Emrys with an apologetic smile. I looked at Dmitriy and Alice who were now whispering. Both appeared curious as to how the conversation would go.

"But, I'm not part of the Bates family," I replied, confused.

"No, but the baby is," he said, taking my hand.

I almost pulled away from his gentle touch, fear penetrating my every thought. Emrys continued to explain: "The curse placed on our family came with a caveat. Its primary goal was to increase our family's paranoia. Over time, we became accustomed to the unknown in regards to the curse. I had no idea you would get pregnant, Khyra. I truly believed the Toxin would have eliminated any possibility. But I suppose magic is more powerful than any man-made creation."

I couldn't look at him; I was so taken aback by his response. For a moment, I felt used and still far too overwhelmed to formulate words. When I remained silent, Emrys continued, as if hoping that'd make me feel better. "Women pregnant with a Bates child on Dmitriy's side would experience an unnatural boost in intelligence and have a desire to invent new things. With my side, pregnant women get prophetic visions—three per trimester."

After he finished his last explanation, the awkward silence began to grow even more. Finally, I asked the question burning in my mind. "What if the child dies? I mean, since we've been in space, every pregnant woman has had a miscarriage. Who's to say the Toxin in my system won't kill the child?"

Dmitriy approached us, his face clouded with concern. "That's the beauty of the curse. The child cannot be killed, except by means of old age."

"Has someone tried?" I asked horrified.

"My mother," he replied solemnly. "She was disgusted at the thought that I might be an abomination. She grew up in a very religious home and didn't agree with our way of life. But, when she tried to abort me, the curse killed her instead. I found this out later in life and hated myself for it. I tried to complete what my mother failed. Every weapon I used either broke or would not work."

An uncomfortable silence filled the room. Judging by the men's expressions, this part of their life never left the two of them.

"We aren't a quarrelsome people, Khyra. Our grandfather was an oddity, and our fathers made certain to continue following in the steps of the Romani people. We might be cursed, but it isn't our curse that forces us to help others beyond our abilities. That is *our* choice," Dmitriy continued, ending on a positive note.

He turned to leave with Alice in the lead when I replied, "For what it's worth, Dmitriy, I'm glad you're here."

He turned back and at first looked a little surprised at my acceptance, then smiled. "Welcome to the family." He gave me a small wink and left the room.

Suddenly, reality hit me. "Oh no—the team! I can only imagine what rumors are being spread about me!"

"Don't worry yourself. I explained everything the moment you fainted. Now, your cousin wants to throttle me, but for now, I think you cleared from his wrath," said Emrys trying to lighten the situation.

"What are people going to say when I have the baby and I show no signs?" I asked, imagining all the rumors that would fly.

"I believe Alice and the Liaisons will take care of that," Emrys assured me. "Now tell me: What did you see?"

I explained my vision in as much detail as possible, and to say he looked worried was an understatement. He tried being positive, saying it would be helpful in planning for the future, but I wished my vision prepared me for the inevitable conversation between John and me.

Grunewald smiled and congratulated me. And as I passed the Liaisons over the course of the next few days, they too said the same. Alice was beyond overjoyed. If she'd had her way, I'm positive she'd throw me a baby shower. Even Colbert gave me a congratulations, in his own weird way. But John, he ... well, he was his usual self, condescending and all.

"I do believe some congratulations are in order," he said stiffly while we were alone on the bridge, stuffing his hands into his uniform pockets.

"Thank you," I said, trying to focus on the map I was slaving over.

"However, I wish you would have told me that you were in a relationship with . . . him," John replied disdainfully.

There it was. John just couldn't say anything kind without putting someone down. "I'm sorry," I said half-heartedly, "I didn't know I needed your permission to fall in love with anyone."

"Khyra, you and that—that *gypsy*—are part of my team. And you are the only family I have left, period. Therefore, it's my business to know about your relationship, whether I agree with it or not!" John replied sternly.

I completely expected that kind of arrogant response. I rolled my eyes, shaking my head in disbelief. "Do you even hear yourself? Not once in that comment did I hear you mention the one hundred thousand people outside this room, all of whom you're supposed to be in charge of. Face it, John: the only thing that you've ever cared about is your reputation, and God forbid anyone gets in the way of that, including family. And you know what? I've heard the stories of how you actually came to be a marshal in the Royal Navy! You aren't too different from my father, bribing people in power to climb your way up that ladder. I can imagine it would sound like a radical idea to you that I actually fall for someone before I let them into my bedroom, instead of just figuring out an angle in which I could use them, like you would."

John gritted his teeth and turned his back to me. He walked to the edge of the room and stared out into the star-filled surroundings. He stood in a militaristic position and shook his head as I strode up beside him. We stood there silently, both our minds probably mulling over the same thing. He hated showing weakness of any kind, and I hated the years of constantly fighting against his ego. To be honest, I often wondered if he hated the fighting too. I tried seeing things from his perspective many times. He didn't have it easy, with his mother's diplomatic position. He was always in the spotlight of the media whenever his mother was pushed at the forefront. Having a superiority complex might have been something that was ingrained in his mind, not something he actually chose. And judging by the next bit of our conversation, I was right.

"Khyra, I don't hate you or your . . . or Emrys. Perhaps I'm envious of your relationship with him. You had the life I always dreamed of—not the rejection part, mind you. And you had the courage and strength to separate yourself from your family and do what you thought was right. That kind of bravery can't be taught through any battle; it's something you're born with." John glanced at me with teary eyes. "You're right; I'm not a leader. Everything I was died back on Earth. I don't proclaim to be psychic, but I think one day you *can* make a difference. And who knows, you might even be a great mother."

I couldn't help but smile at his last comment. "Who knows—maybe together we can make a difference."

We both turned to find the team had silently entered sometime during our conversation. The men pretended to go about their duties, but it didn't take a genius to realize they'd heard the majority. I laughed—and suddenly found myself doubled over with that all-too-familiar headache. Emrys had found ways of stretching his abilities to minimize the pain, but this time it felt different. I didn't see the usual vision but strange planets, unlike anything I'd ever dreamed of. There were four. One was encased in darkness, another surrounded by light, the third an Earth-like planet, and the last, a tiny one covered in greenery. Each one flashed in my head as if they were all equally important.

These worlds were foreign and terrifying, to say nothing of the strange creatures that would accompany each planet. I knew this was a full vision, but it didn't last as long as the first; I came to, possibly within minutes. I found myself sitting on the floor of the bridge, with Emrys's arms wrapped around me. I felt comforted there, but then Colbert tried to be funny and lighten the mood.

"What did the magical baby tell you?"

I didn't take offense to his comment—in any other situation I would've laughed. But my mind was too focused on the planets. Almost everyone else gave him a disapproving look, but to their surprise, I responded without a hint of sarcasm. "I think he was trying to show me our new home. I saw four planets, which I assume are within the same solar system. But I also sensed some kind of danger."

This was the first time I'd revealed to anyone other than Emrys and Dmitriy about what I saw. The three of us had felt it best to not worry the others, especially since we didn't fully understand the meaning behind the panic in the first vision.

"Wait, how do you know the gender of your child?" asked Grunewald.

"It's a special gift mothers of Bates children have. It's a deeper connection than most expecting mothers," said Emrys with an admiring look.

"Well, if these planets are to be our new home, let us hope the danger is minimal," said John encouragingly.

I was now in my second trimester. The pain eventually disappeared, but the constant visions were just as annoying. I went about my duties helping the people and the team. Unfortunately, due to my condition, I was unable to do everything no matter how hard I tried. But that's when the group started acting like a team. Everyone doubled up on their responsibilities to help, and I'd like to think we grew closer from that.

My third vision came when I was seven months pregnant. But it felt so disconnected from the other two—at that time, that is. I continuously saw the yin-yang symbol. It was nice in a way; somehow it reminded me that we all needed to have balance in our lives. As relaxing as this concept was, I still couldn't stop dwelling on the first vision. When would it come? Would we even know, or, like the Toxin, would it be unexpected? These concerns soon left around my eighth month, when the baby began to move more than normal. According to Alice, I wasn't showing any signs of delivering prematurely—the fetus and my body were both right where they should've been in the normal development stage, so it made me wonder if something was about to happen.

The mass departure vision came unexpectedly as I'd feared, and the reason for it was nothing I could've guessed.

I ran down the hall toward the bridge and to be honest, I don't quite remember why—perhaps it was a new discovery with Alice's research that I'd wanted to share. But whatever the reason, it was quickly shoved to the side when I stepped into the room and came to an abrupt halt. The portal from my hallucination stood menacingly in front of us. And just like in my vision, we hovered over a new planet.

"Why have we stopped?" I asked, avoiding the obvious.

"Good news: we found a habitable planet. Bad news: it's the last one in the galaxy," said Colbert.

"We're at the edge of the galaxy?" I asked nervously.

"The very edge, in fact," the scientist continued, "from what the maps have shown us. We're at the very tip of the outer arm of the galaxy. I assume if there's a big swirling vortex of doom at this tip, other arms might have a similar one."

"So the string theory was right?" I mused, recalling the different dimensions of Earth one learns about in high school physics.

"Whoa, hold it. I never said this was a doorway to another dimension," Colbert exclaimed, horrified at my assumption.

"No, but I did. Or at the very least, my first vision did," I confessed.

"You foresaw this moment?" asked John, sounding mildly offended that I hadn't confided in him.

"I just saw the map, a portal, and this arguing," I lied.

"Look, I refuse to fly into some portal that a psychic baby gave you in a vision. The planet below is perfect for us!" exclaimed Colbert, seeing where this was going. "Besides, you don't even know if you'll survive after going through the portal!"

"No one's making you go, Andrew," snapped John. "Khyra, is that portal really the way to the planets you believe are our ultimate destination?"

"There's only one way to find out," I replied as confidently as I could.

"I can't believe I'm listening to this. I'm leaving, and I'm taking as many people as I can with me," replied Colbert, storming out of the room.

I stayed on the bridge while the other team members raced after Colbert. It was the last I saw of him, or the twenty thousand other people that followed his lead. I imagined he survived and had a long life, but whether Jacob and James Colbert, the masked bullies Amber met, were Andrew's descendants, is impossible to know.

To my amazement, Colbert was the only one of the core team that left. Even half of the Liaisons believed whatever Emrys and Dmitriy told them. I was grateful for their faith in me, but I was so afraid I was leading them to their doom. Silently, I went to the manual controls. And as Dmitriy turned off the "New Earth" tracker, I guided the ship toward the portal until we felt the force of it sucking us in.

Our equipment rattled and bright lights flashed as we entered uncharted territories. I can't exactly say what happened to us in the portal, or even if it transported us to another time or dimension. But I can tell you what happened when we exited. After the blinding lights faded, we noticed the ship had stopped moving. I stood and glanced out the window to see a beautiful elliptical galaxy—billions of stars and planets adding their own unique colors.

"Khyra, we have a problem," said Dmitriy.

I turned around to see that the map that had guided us for the last six years was no longer functioning. Only a single dot in the middle of it revealed our location in the vast unknown. We were officially alone, with no idea where to go.

"Well, all we can do is push forward. Let's see what that galaxy has in store for us," I replied, pointing to the mass of stars and planets.

"This is your discovery, your vision. That being said, I think it only fitting that you give our new discoveries a name," said John kindly.

"What's this galaxy going to be called?" asked Lukas, agreeing with John.

I stared out the window, completely mesmerized by the beauty. Then, suddenly, an overwhelming thought came to me. *Time*; there was something about this galaxy that seemed different, almost magical. The name that came to me rolled off my tongue.

"Chronosalis."

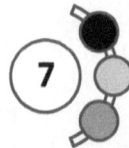

7

As soon as that word escaped my lips, I was reminded that I carried a magical child. The name of the galaxy seemed to spark something—as if my baby had only been waiting for me to say that very word before making his entrance into the world. I don't recall much of the birth, sadly. The visions I had during my pregnancy seemed to rail against the walls of my mind. But I definitely remember hearing my son's first cries—that's not something I could forget. And when Alice placed him in my arms, I said, with tears in my eyes, hello to my son, Owen.

Emrys was an amazing father, and often took Owen around to see everyone and even play with buttons on the bridge that were no longer active. Naturally, the citizens were very confused about the newcomer, but Alice and the remaining Liaisons were well on top of things. They'd already planned for this. Alice had finally found a formula giving the people a higher chance of combating the effects of the Toxin that had previously prevented them from having children.

Within two months, we were on the edge of the Chronosalis galaxy. I half expected the planets from my vision to suddenly appear, but we came upon them slowly. With the altered technology, compliments of Dmitriy's ideas, we were able to see these planets from a sizable distance. But as I studied their makeups, I discovered something disturbing. Their landmasses—or rather, what I could see on the map—changed rather frequently, as if they were living, moving things. I noticed a very small planet just outside of the solar system, and knew it to be part of the original system at one time. Upon closer examination of the planet's surface, large sections of the land seemed damaged. My best guess was that a massive asteroid had knocked the planet slightly out of orbit, and it had been floating nearby ever since. But that may have been thousands of years ago for all I knew. Nevertheless, these planets soon became known as Diraetus, Darmentraea, Galaseya, and the lone one, Heirsha.

I expressed my concerns to the team members that we probably should wait to explore these planets until we knew more, but everyone was tired of being in the ship. They thought my concerns were unwarranted; after all, Owen had guided us here. By the time we reached landing distance of the three planets, our ship just stopped: we couldn't move forward even an inch. It was as if something was holding us there. This just added to the list of my growing concerns.

I silently scoffed at the "New Earth" meetings we had. Everyone, including the remaining civilians, agreed to keep small reminders of Earth. Calendar dates, time, and even our surnames in honor of the fallen. This was admirable and would even be slightly poetic if it weren't for my constant warnings. But then, John so kindly reminded me of how hypocritical I sounded. I'd begged them to go through the portal based on a hallucination, and now that we were at the next vision, I was hesitant. And as much as I hated to admit it, he was right. But at the same time, something bothered me greatly about our new discovery.

The rest of this part of the story has been told before. Our ship rapidly broke down and families split apart due to the unexpected escape, but there were also terrible last words exchanged. I knew the planets had something to do with our ship breaking down, and as much as we'd stocked the pods full of supplies, we just weren't prepared. It was at the very last possible second that we all realized the planets were truly the cause of our demise. Strange colored forcefields tore the ship apart, bringing the debris down onto Diraetus and Darmentraea as if the worlds themselves were deciding what piece of us they wanted.

Panicked, we all bolted to the pods, knowing full well that each pod might be claimed by one planet, splitting up and destroying families. Now, I've made plenty of mistakes in the two thousand years I've been alive, but this next moment is, by far, my biggest regret. I held Owen tightly as we were about to follow Emrys into a pod. He held out a hand to help me into the pod as John came rushing around the corner straight toward me.

"Khyra! I'm so glad I found you! Come with me—that pod is too full, and there's plenty of room in the next one!" John urged, grabbing my free arm.

I shrugged him off, not entirely sure I wanted to follow someone whom I'd *just* settled old grievances with. I looked at Emrys, who stared at John angrily. Although he worked with John and had known him for many, many years, he'd still never fully trusted him.

"John, I can't leave my family," I said, gesturing to Emrys and the child in my arms.

"But I'm your family too!" he exclaimed. When he realized how selfish that sounded, John quickly changed his tone. "We . . . we're all family—we can all go in together!"

"Then come with us! There's still room for one more, John," suggested Emrys, although to me it sounded like more of a challenge.

John peered into the pod and I could have sworn a horrific expression flashed across his face, the red flashing lights of the ship accenting his emotions. That's when I knew: he just wanted to find more ways of controlling me, just as he had when we were children. Despite the fact that the rest of our family was dead, somewhere in his twisted and arrogant mind, he still wanted to preserve that reputation they strived so hard to maintain.

"No, I'm done, John—"

"Khyra, listen to me!" he interrupted.

"You're in no position to control anything, John! We're trying to preserve the human race, not our reputation, which in case you haven't noticed, died along with Earth! I'm going in this pod and if you won't join us like a true family, then I want nothing else to do with you!" I exclaimed. As a scientist, I don't generally read into a lot of things, especially emotions, but I swear I saw a tear fall from his cheek. He nodded, sorrow filling his face as he reluctantly turned and headed back to the pod of his choice. I didn't know until much later that my response completely broke him.

As for where the people went, Grunewald went to Darmentraea along with most of the Russians and

Germans—a few Americans slipped in too, I think. Dmitriy went along too, and he later became the patriarch of Rydan's family. Emrys was heartbroken to be separated from his cousin, but everyone was in such a panic and hurry that I'm sure Dmitriy was trying to look for his only family, but accidentally got into the wrong pod. Emrys and I, along with all the Liaisons voyaged to Diraetus. A variety of nationalities came along with us, which helped make this new planet feel more like home in a way. But Alice and John, with almost all the citizens of the United Kingdom, mostly British scientists, journeyed to Galaseya.

Now the planets we all landed on weren't our first choices. It was just as the team had feared: the planets grabbed onto our pods and took their pick. The vessels were made to hold a good several thousand people, maybe even more. Each consisted of at least three levels, and there were bunks and bathrooms, food supplies—basically, we could have lived in it for a long time if needed. Even though the pods were durable, they weren't ready for the power of a force field. They started rattling as the unusual force pulled us in, creating a bizarre turbulence. I held Owen close as Emrys held us both in his arms. If I were going to die, I'd rather be with the people I love, rather than my estranged cousin.

Our pod came to a slow stop rather than a crash landing as we'd all expected. Considering everything we had been through, this was a nice surprise. Some strong men wrenched open the door and a bright light instantly blinded us. We stumbled out of the pod. As our eyes adjusted, we took in the surrounding sites. I really don't know what I was expecting Diraetus to look like, but an eerie replica of Earth, pre-industry, was not it. And judging by the others' expressions, they thought the same thing.

There's no denying it was strange, but there was a certain surreal beauty to it all. We'd landed gently in a massive field full of luscious grass and wildflowers of various colors. Surrounding the picture-perfect field were skyscraper-high tall trees. Some looked similar to pine trees, but the majority had yet to be identified. But the perfume that both the trees and flowers emitted was a mixture of fruit with a hint of lavender. All of it was unbelievable, to say nothing of the towering mountains in the distance that had yet to be explored. Of all the people on the doomed *Beacon*, I felt we had it made. But that selfish thought made my heart ache for my cousin and the others we'd left behind. My gaze wandered up to the sky, and it was the sight of Darmentraea and Galaseya that would be a constant reminder we were no longer on Earth.

So here we were in the year one A.E. (after Earth), making this field our base camp. We scoured the land in shifts, looking for water, edible plants, and signs of animal life. From what we observed, there weren't many differences from Earth. We found deer, bear, wild cats, and coyotes. But all the animals tried to avoid us, the newcomers.

We collected materials from the woods and made homes out of them. At first, they were more like lean-tos, but eventually, we made more proper structures. On one of our searches, we found a location where pieces of the *Beacon* had crash-landed. It was nice to incorporate materials from home. This took a few months to do, and it was during these trips that we sometimes found strange brown lights surrounding the metal. At first, some thought it was a chemical reaction to something in the atmosphere, but I was more inclined to believe it was something we didn't want to mess with.

As a population, we got along miraculously well, and once we established a civilization, it was almost unanimous that the people deemed Emrys and I as the leaders. We didn't like the idea of leading although we accepted the position; we made sure to stay humble and not let it get to our heads, and we raised Owen in the same manner.

He was the oldest of the second generation and years later, when others had children of their own, they instinctively wanted to follow him. It gave us a hope we had forgotten. Hope for humanity.

As we toiled to establish our civilization, we started seeing more and more of those strange brown lights. It's like they were spies for a mystical force. It grew so disturbing that eventually we made it a priority to find the source. Owen was almost a year old by the time Emrys and I went out in search of these lights. Normally, we would've gathered our hunters and explorers, but Emrys's gift warned him not to bring along a large crowd. I joked with him that we would be saving time if his visions had said what the lights were. But even I knew psychic visions of any kind were never clear.

We traveled miles away from base camp into the dense forest when we came across a most out-of-place and unusual configuration. A beautiful, towering glass structure lay before us. If it weren't for the trees and leaf-strewn ground, I'd have thought we'd discovered a city on Earth. But the thousands of small brown lights floating around the structure brought us back to Diraetus. Emrys and I exchanged nervous glances as we silently crept around the building until we found an entrance. Naturally, we thought this was a setup, especially when the front doors opened for us.

"We should head back now," said Emrys nervously.

I was going to agree with him, but just as I was turning my head, the few little brown lights became dozens and shaped themselves into a group of fifteen glowing humans. Terrified, I replied, "I don't think we have much of a choice."

Emrys stole a quick glance behind him and stared at the light people as if mesmerized. Blindly, he grabbed my hand and with our attention on the potential danger in front of us, started forward. I expected to see a lobby and a few elevators to lead to the upper floors. But within moments, I found myself alone, tied to a chair in an interrogation room. My only company was my captor: a beautiful woman dressed in strange white robes. Her pale hands were folded patiently in front of her, and her dark brown hair fell in waves past her shoulders.

"Where is Emrys? What have you done with him?" I demanded, struggling against my bindings.

"The male is safe for now," said the woman, emotionless.

"What do you want?" I spat.

The woman held up one index finger, the tip glowing brown. She made a flickering motion toward my face, and a burning sensation grew on my lower jaw. I felt warm, sticky, blood drip down my neck. She got what she wanted: my undivided attention.

"You're in no position to ask questions, Khyra," the woman replied as she started circling me like a vulture. "Now, so that we don't waste our time, I'm just going to ask a simple question. Why are you on our planet?"

If it were any other human or creature asking me this, generally I'd snap back, but this woman already proved her disinterest in my safety. So, I politely said, "My people were in danger, and we needed to find a new planet."

"And you thought our planet would be the perfect candidate?" she shot back.

"I'm getting the feeling that this won't be our first conversation, so can I at least know your name?" I asked, hoping to change the topic.

The woman let out a series of whistles and shot a coy smile at me as she replied, "That is my name in our language. I suppose the closest translation in your tongue would be, Hannah."

I shook my head, their strange form of ESP really got to me as that was the name of a childhood bully. "Look, Hannah, we weren't interested in landing on any planet in this solar system. We were honestly just passing through."

Another wound opened on my arm as Hannah replied, "My siblings and I could remove you from our world and eject you back into space. We would feel no remorse. I suggest you show me a little more respect, Child of Earth," hissed the creature. "But, I suppose we could still use you. Provide that you speak not nor even hint of this meeting to anyone . . . or we will find out."

"Wait, what *are* you?" I asked hesitantly.

Hannah put her face practically five inches from mine and grabbed my face. "In essence, *we* are the planet you infiltrated, and you will pay for your crimes!"

She released her grip and stepped back as all ten fingers began glowing. She formed her fingers into the shape of a claw and proceeded to slice me. When she was satisfied with her handiwork, Hannah wrenched my face to the side so hard my magical binding loosened, and I was suddenly on the floor of the hut I shared with Emrys and Owen. The ground beneath me vibrated as my arrival stirred quite the commotion. I slowly rose from the ground, surprisingly sensing no pain as Emrys rushed to my side.

"Sweetheart, what happened?" he exclaimed, effortlessly lifting me off the ground.

I still felt dazed by the whole ordeal, but I couldn't risk revealing who my captors were at this time. As far as I knew they were part of the planet, but their power was unimaginable.

"I don't remember," I lied, casting my eyes down.

"How can you not remember getting all these marks?" said the camp physician, who'd rushed in when the vibrations at my arrival had started.

Somehow all the wounds Hannah had inflicted healed completely, leaving only faded scars. My body was free of bloodstains.

"I must've gotten lost in the woods on my way back," I said, knowing Emrys would try to pry answers out of me.

Fortunately, he left the topic alone for a few weeks, mostly because a huge storm nearly swept up our camp. But when he did, we were in bed, listening to the pitter-patter of small woodland critters outside.

"Khyra, why won't you tell me what happened in the glass tower?" his voice came in the dark, "One minute you were right next to me, the next—gone! I searched everywhere for you, but I didn't even see a sign of those glowing lights. I tried getting into the tower, but it was sealed. Then that disappeared and my only thought was that perhaps you were lost and made your way back to the camp. Please, Sweetheart, why won't you tell me?"

"Because I don't know what would happen if I did," I whispered, staring down at my bruised hands.

Emrys sat up in bed. Darmentraea shone on his face, casting harsh shadows that only accented his concern. "Are you in danger?"

I sat up as the light graced my scarred face. I glanced at Owen's crib, his soft cooing contrasting the dismal mood. A tear fell down my cheek as a wave of reality swept over me. I looked at Emrys and finally said, "We all are."

"Khyra . . . your scars, they're—they're bleeding!" Emrys exclaimed, reaching for a cloth to staunch the blood.

Just as before, my wounds were opened and pain spread throughout my whole body before I was dragged away by an unseen force.

"I thought we discussed this. Our meeting was our secret!" Hannah's voice rang through the near-empty room.

Yet again I was tied to a chair, blood pooling at my feet. "I didn't say anything about you!" I protested weakly.

"Not directly. But the terms of your release were that you were not to warn your humans or even hint at the possibility of a problem. You broke these terms. Therefore, your scars returned you to me. Do you understand how this works?"

It was at this moment that I realized what she meant. These scars were her sadistic version of a prison; invisible chains of bondage that gave me just enough room to move around. I hung my head low, having no choice but concede to whatever these creatures demanded.

"Wonderful!" exclaimed Hannah, seeing I had given in. "Now that you understand your role, we will proceed with . . . learning more about your kind."

I wanted to ask what she meant, but I had no time before dozens of beings surrounded me, casting powerful, brown beams of light. I was engulfed almost immediately, and all my Earth memories seemed to race through my mind. This unusual torture method must have continued for twenty minutes before Hannah called above my screeches of pain: "She's had enough for now. We don't want to kill her just yet."

I peered through half-closed eyes, daring to see what my captors planned. But I just saw low-lying shrubs and trunks of massive trees. Light from Galaseya gave the surrounding woods such a severe yet peaceful look. I lifted my sore body and found myself at the forest's edge. Home lay right in front of me. Laughter and joy wafted through the air; apparently, some didn't realize I had been missing.

With my headache and sore body bearable, I clambered to my feet and started toward camp, trying to think of another excuse to feed Emrys. I slipped behind buildings and clung to the shadows hoping my strange behavior would go unnoticed, but a strong grip covered my mouth from behind and spun me around.

"Khyra, it's me. Relax!" said Emrys in a panicked whisper.

He looked around to be sure we were alone and slowly he brought me to the soft ground. He held my hands in silence, his dark eyes grew wide. "What have they done to you?"

"I don't know what you mean," I said honestly, my lungs noticeably sore from all of my screams.

Cautiously, Emrys revealed to me the truth: "I know about the creatures, Diraetus, and they tortured you into not saying anything."

Emrys was a genius! He found a loophole in Hannah's demands! I scoped out the surrounding field and nearby buildings, terrified the creatures were lurking nearby. Playing on his loophole, I replied, "There's no way you could've known that."

A group of people passed close to our hiding spot. I held my breath as Emrys took my hand and we walked farther into the field, away from curious onlookers.

"My father made it his mission in life to understand magic of all sorts. He discovered that it exists all around because magic resides on its own plane. I never fully believed him until we came here. When we made Diraetus our home, I noticed my abilities growing stronger. It was like I had this freedom to extend them beyond what I could on Earth," Emrys explained. "So, I continued practicing my gifts and while you slept, I would gather bits of information from you."

"I'm glad I don't feel so alone. But nothing can be . . ."

Emrys covered my mouth, his expression warning me that I was still bound by Hannah. "Don't worry, my love, I will always be here for you," he whispered, leaning in for a kiss. When our lips met, an electric shock coursed through my body. The vibration energized me, making me feel empowered. It was as if everything Hannah and her followers did was forever altered in that moment in time.

"Trust me," he murmured into my ear so quietly I barely heard him, "those things . . . those *scientists* have another think coming. They won't be experimenting on you again. I have a plan."

And that's how their name came to be. Over the next several years, I was kidnapped at various times, but they never suspected Emrys's plan. Of course, I didn't either, exactly, but it was better this way—that way, they couldn't leach the information out of my memories against my will.

At the time, I wished I understood why I got that shock wave every time Emrys and I touched. On Owen's fifteenth birthday, I finally had my answer when I was swept away yet again.

I arrived in that all-too-familiar chair with blood pooling at my feet. The Scientists surrounded me in their usual circle with Hannah in front of me, looking smugger than ever. I braced myself for the inevitable pain as they struck me with their torturous power. But nothing came. Not even a tickle! I looked around at the Scientists, who looked as confused as I felt. Suddenly, a powerful urge rose up in me. I can only describe it in one word: freedom. The look of horror on Hannah's face was the last thing I saw before I broke free from my chains of bondage.

"Mom, Mom, can you hear me?" Owen's voice echoed.

I opened my eyes to see my son and husband hovering over me, concern written all over their faces.

"I . . . I beat them!" I said, stunned.

"Dad, what is she talking about?" asked Owen, panic lacing his voice.

Emrys asked Owen to finish his chores and begrudgingly, he did.

"Why do you say that?" Emrys whispered to me, his voice full of uncertainty.

"My scars—they aren't bleeding, for one. And, I'm still here!" I exclaimed, finally able to fully appreciate the concept of freedom.

"Then it worked!" he beamed, opening his arms wide to pull me close.

"Wait! What?" I pushed my hands against his chest, eyeing him suspiciously. "What did you do?"

"When you came back from your first meeting with them, I sensed magic within you. Planet magic, if you will. I knew they were picking your brain for memories of Earth. But in doing so, they made a mistake," he replied with a sly smile.

"A mistake?" I repeated. "What kind of mistake?"

"They infused you with their magic," he replied with a devious grin. "Every time they entered your mind, they left a bit of residual magic. So, each time we touched, I merely connected the residue like a puzzle in hopes that one day you'd be free from their grasp."

"So, what you're saying is, I have magical powers now," I said slowly, not even able to believe my own words.

"It's only temporary," Emrys assured me.

"Really?" I asked doubtfully.

Without meeting my gaze, Emrys sheepishly replied, "No . . . actually, I have no idea how long your magic will last or what you can do. What I did was experimental; it's never been done before. Earth had some magic, but this planet, and maybe the others, are very close to the plane that magic resides on. Anything could happen, I suppose."

Emrys always rambled when he was nervous or afraid of what I'd say. I used to find it cute, but given the circumstances, now it was mildly annoying. When he noticed I wasn't too impressed with his answer, he continued in a different tone. "But you're not in this alone. I will help you every step of the way and now that we've held the Scientists back, we can tell Owen. He deserves to know after all these years of secrecy."

Owen took the news quite well, actually. We should've known this, as he inherited his father's gift and knew that Diraetus held dangers of sorts. He understood our continued need for secrecy. The Scientists never harmed the people directly. We wanted it to stay that was as oftentimes knowing the truth could potentially be more dangerous. Owen promised to keep this all in the family. And as for my magic—well, it was definitely a learning process. It began with visions, but not of day to day life. This had a futuristic feel to it. Sometimes I could read others' thoughts. But these two elements weren't the weirdest. The wild animals that had always shied away from us would now often come right up to me. Fast-forward to the present, and everyone knows what I can do. But at the beginning, I solely relied on the power of my mind to instinctively guide me in learning these new magical skills. As a family, we practiced our abilities and tried to strengthen them, but nearly every time we did this, we would see flashes of small brown lights in the distance. The Scientists, showing themselves enough to remind us that they were watching, and they weren't going to give up so easily.

In fact, the day they struck back was not only full of terror, but futuristic irony. It was two years after I'd broken free from my prison—sometime in the autumn, if I recall correctly. Owen and I were in our house. I hadn't seen Emrys all day, as earlier he'd gone on a hunting trip with some of the others. When night came and the hunting party returned, both Owen and I grew concerned when the men and women said Emrys had wanted to explore an area in the woods and had struck out on his own. Between their vague response and Emrys's unusual behavior, I knew the Scientists were behind his disappearance. Fortunately, some of the people pointed me in the right direction.

Owen and I packed the necessities and started off for the forest. We wove in between trees, climbed hills, and waded through rivers for hours. The morning light peeked through the trees as we came to a clearing. Does this sound familiar? It should, because this was the same place where two thousand years later, I enacted my vengeance on the Scientists. Why so symbolic? It does sound rather dramatic, I'll admit. But it was to make a point—one that I wanted them to fear.

When Owen and I entered the clearing, the Scientists, along with beings embodying the other two planets, stood in front of us. Emrys knelt in the middle, bound and weary.

"Dad!" my son exclaimed, prepared to rescue Emrys. I held him back and stared Hannah down, ignoring the curious gazes of the other planets.

"You've left us alone for two years. What could you possibly want now?" I asked, showing no signs of fear.

"You let her speak to you like that?" asked a man from Darmentraea.

"Thank you for the commentary, Martheykos," said Hannah, annoyed. "Khyra and I have a special relationship, don't we?"

"If by *relationship* you mean torture victim, then sure!" I spat.

Khyra, don't antagonize them further. It will only make things worse! Emrys warned telepathically.

"What does she mean by torture?" asked a woman from Galaseya.

"Humans are rather emotional creatures who often misuse words in a state of fear," another Scientist replied.

"I suppose," said the Galaseyan creature suspiciously.

"Okay, can we wrap this up? Petraylin and I have things to do, you know . . . people to fry," Martheykos said nonchalantly.

"Quite right," Hannah agreed. "Khyra, we are eternally grateful to you and your kind for arriving in our planetary system. Our worlds were in danger of total destruction, because the Balance that we thrive on hung by a thread. Your husband understood our crisis and has offered himself to become one with the Balance. Because of his sacrifice, we can all live peacefully!"

This elaborate lie was so convincing that the other planets bought it! The last telepathic message Emrys sent me before the planets combined their powers to throw him to another realm was: *Fight back, Khyra. And don't you give up until you defeat them! I love you!*

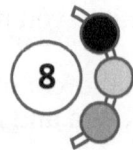

8

My life was officially over at that moment. I lost the love of my life, and I had no idea where they sent him. I wanted to believe this Balance Hannah had mentioned in her lie to the other planets really existed, but I had no proof and no reason to trust that it did. Leading the people became impossible, even with Owen's stern dedication. Fortunately, I had close friends who were willing to step up. As far as our people knew, Emrys was mauled by a bear.

As the years passed, I had to isolate myself from my people, as they didn't know what had happened to me . . . and I wasn't getting any older. Fortunately, during my mortal life, I'd aged quite well and had always looked younger than I was, but when you've been around for fifty years and you still look barely forty, people start asking questions. But the isolation wasn't so bad. I found solace deep in the woods, and I felt closer to Emrys there, in a morbid sort of way. Owen visited with me as much as time allowed. But even he had to move on. He found love and had three children, two girls and a boy. He even found a way to suppress his children's gifts just so they didn't become a threat to the planets.

But his efforts proved useless as the Scientists began twisting the minds of my people, including my descendants. Fortunately, my grandchildren and their offspring could occasionally see through the manipulations, and saw glimpses of the truth, literally and metaphorically. See, the Scientists used the information of our home planet that they'd stolen from me, and every generation born fell under the same spell, believing they were living on Earth. Everything changed—and I do mean everything. People began to see the world as Earth when civilization began there, at least for the most part. Sometimes, for their personal fun, the Scientists would fast-forward the spell, and people would think they were in the Dark Ages one day and the Renaissance period the next. I can imagine it gave Owen a headache, as his magic allowed him to see beyond the Mask. As the generations progressed, they started Earth's religions and other beliefs all over again. The Mask soon washed away our initial system of marriage, which was mostly an unspoken vow rather than an entire ceremony, similar to that of Galaseya.

Now this information that the Scientists had received from me was not entirely what the Mask was made of. From the sounds of it, they had been spying on every one of the Diraetans over the years, and gleaned information from them as well.

After seeing how much had changed, I lost hope and just found no reason to fight. I used my gifts to conceal myself from the Scientists, but after a while, I was dead to them. And they disappeared into the background, continuing their secret rule over the planet. There was no immediate battle to be won, and the visions I received were useless. Until, that is, twenty years after Emrys's disappearance, when I had an unusual visit.

It was dusk, and I was just about to leave my little woodland hut when I heard the weirdest noise. It sounded like wind whistling through chimes. But as I turned to close my back door. Pure silence. Usually, some kind of creature would make a small greeting sound, but it was as if something had scared them all away. When I turned around, I too, almost fled. The women from Galaseya were there to pay me a visit. Despite my immortality, I felt far too old to be dealing with their planetary drama.

"Please, I don't want any trouble. I just want to be left in peace," I said pitifully.

"We mean you no harm, Khyra," said one woman kindly. "Please allow us to introduce ourselves. The humans on our world call us the Sidhe. My name is Levendria, and this is Vaeris and Analira. We have come to apologize for our actions."

"I don't understand," I replied honestly.

"We were under the false impression that your people offered your lover as a way of restoring our Balance. Diraetus lied to us," said Analira.

"And it took you twenty years to figure that out?" I asked bitterly.

"We cannot fathom the pain you have felt all these years, but we wish to make it right," Vaeris explained.

"Bring Emrys back then," I challenged.

"Regretfully, we cannot. Emrys dwells on the Balance plane, the realm that keeps our worlds in order. He has now become part of it. Without them both, we will surely cease to exist. Diraetus had no right to deceive us and damage the Balance even more," Levendria replied.

"So how do you intend to repay me?" I asked, beginning to doubt their every word.

"It is true we cannot return Emrys to you, but he *is* still alive. And it is our belief that restoring the Balance will bring him back," said Levendria. "We were never meant to become humanoid. But the other planets envied your form, and if something occurs with one planet, the others must follow. Only when we are returned to the planet itself will the Balance be restored; until then, Darmentraea and Diraetus will wreak havoc."

I chewed on their words for a moment.

"We believe you can return us to the planet," she finished.

It was a lot for them to ask, especially after all I had been through. I brought my attention back to the beings in front of me and said, "Why is this daunting task solely up to me?"

"You are immortal, and part Diraetus. You are the true Protector of this planet—surely you must've had unusual visions?" asked Analira.

I reflected on the visions that I'd intentionally ignored for years. The Balance was prominent among them, but mostly it came in the visual of that familiar yin-yang symbol. But other visions came periodically where I saw silhouettes of two boys and a girl, all three representing the elements of earth, fire, and water. I considered what the Sidhe had said about me being the Protector of Diraetus. This meant there would be more protectors like me in the future.

"Khyra?" Vaeris called my attention.

"Yes, sorry," I stuttered. "I've had visions of your Balance and vague images of future people like me. But I have no idea when they're to arrive or who they are."

"I believe we can shed light on that conundrum," said Levendria with a smile. "The only ones strong enough to become like you are those of the Bates line."

This answer made no sense at first, but then I remember what Emrys told me all those years ago. All magic resided on a different plane. I had magic and because of the Balance, so would the other three people in my visions. The only conclusion that it all came to was that they'd be Emrys's or Dmitriy's descendants, although the latter seemed impossible at the time since we had no idea what became of Dmitriy.

I eventually agreed to work with the Sidhe. Levendria replied, "Now, all we can do is patiently and vigilantly wait. The three people will come."

As my relationship with the Sidhe progressed, they informed me about the happenings on their world. I came to find out that my cousin could no longer handle the pressures of restarting a civilization and had ended his life. They assured me that they'd tried to stop him, but John was not one to be deterred when he set his mind on something. Although he did have a relatively peaceful life and even had a family, I never stopped wondering if his suicide had something to do with our last meeting. That was something even the Sidhe couldn't answer for me.

My mortal life may have been done, but my immortal life had just begun. It's at this part of the story that Amber's family rose up. But it didn't have to be them. Emrys's and Dmitriy's line branched out wide. Anyone could have been the three people from my vision. But I began relying on these apparitions so much that they were no longer prophetic but self-fulfilling. See, I enlisted an innocent family in a war that wasn't exactly theirs to fight. All because of a vague assumption that Emrys might be alive after it was all over.

Five hundred years, that's how long I had to wait before even a sign showed itself. And as usual, it came in the form of something I never expected. The Sidhe told me of unusual activity occurring on Darmentraea. Somehow, over the centuries, Emrys had learned how to manipulate the Balance to spy on the planets undetected. He'd overheard my plans with the Sidhe and kept a close eye on those the Sidhe or I couldn't. Eventually, Emrys found a way to telepathically communicate with us. He had almost total control. Between the Sidhe and Emrys, I received so much telepathic information of exact details that I felt like I was there watching everyone! I remember as a child hearing stories of God in the Bible and how he was all knowing. It wasn't an easy concept for me to grasp, but now that I was semi-omniscient through these telepathic communications, I finally understood why only an all-powerful deity could know everything. It wasn't a task meant for a simple immortal.

Now, all the planets have heard the tales of the supernatural family, but there are some stories even they don't know—secrets that essentially made them who they are. And it all began with Rydan Bates, a direct descendant of Dmitriy. Like his ancestors, Rydan had the gift of technology. But living on a dark planet that altered the very nature of a human being caused all of Dmitriy's ancestors to have their own unique power related to technology. Rydan was no exception—in fact, he was *more* special. Any invention that he envisioned, he could make. It was quite fascinating and he loved it. His talent became his comfort on Darmentraea. The Brothers had nearly eradicated his family, with the exception of a few who not only hid their gifts but later married into the Grunewald family. Yes, one Grunewald was born with Bates blood: Kylis. In fact, he was the only one. As the original story goes, the Grunewald and Oak families on Galaseya only had the same bloodline due to Rydan's invention which I will explain more in detail shortly.

According to Emrys, who made it his mission to watch and protect the people of Darmentraea, Rydan was orphaned at a young age, much like many of the planet's children. Rydan spent most of his childhood either running from the rogue Darmentraeans or the Brothers. He hated having to conceal his gifts, and wished he could escape. His wish was granted when he was just fourteen years old. Martheykos had grown tired of chasing Rydan, and became fearful the human would find a way to overthrow him. So, in true Martheykos fashion, the evil tyrant rid himself of the young teenager by casting him to Galaseya. From what Emrys gathered, Rydan didn't remember too much from his landing, just blinding colorful lights and waking up to find himself surrounded by a few curious beasts of the woods. The Brothers figured that at least in this world, Rydan would truly feel loneliness. They weren't wrong—that's how things were at first. The Sidhe watched the young man as Rydan struggled to adjust to the bright and cheery atmosphere, and discreetly, they guided him to a secluded area of Galaseya where he could acclimate. They even provided a stone home for him to start his life. But Rydan couldn't care less about starting over. He was so bent on revenge against the Brothers that at the age of sixteen he created a strange fruit in hopes of gaining more power. He had been working on this experiment for much longer than was originally believed. Most of his time consisted of trial and error, but soon his idea came to fruition. This fruit gave him exactly what he wanted and more. It altered his DNA so much that his brown eyes turned silver and his original power had no limitations. He could take simple tools and recreate them to make any invention. But the transformation he went through took much energy out of him.

With his new godlike powers, Rydan continued his mission of stopping the Brothers. But an unusual encounter caused Rydan to put everything on hold. He fell in love. Kraenia Sullivan was her name, and she loved every aspect of who Rydan was, even his unusual abilities. Unfortunately, their time together was short, as she passed away during childbirth, two years after their relationship began.

When his daughter, Saraleast, was four, she became afflicted by the genetic Toxin disease that had killed so many before her. Many believed she became ill due to the nature of her Darmentraean blood combined with the Galaseyan atmosphere, as was common for the two opposing cultures. That could not be further from the truth. Galaseya has and always will have a certain healing aspect to it, which is why very little sickness occurs among the people. That, however, didn't stop the Toxin from rearing its ugly head, and there was no way of curing it, as the treatment to lessen its effects died with the ship. But Rydan couldn't lose the only thing important in his life. He altered the fruit he created those many years ago and added his blood, thinking it might be a good healing agent.

He got more than he bargained for.

As the rest of the story goes, Saraleast lived, and obtained a wonderful power. The Sidhe, Emrys, and I all agreed that this was our first sign of my visions coming to fruition. We were all so hopeful, until Rydan tried to destroy the fruit. The Sidhe had it in their mind that we needed this creation to produce more possibilities of the magical hero we were all waiting for. But Emrys and I didn't agree. We initially wanted to be distant observers and let things unfold as they should, for the most part.

But despite their best intentions, the Sidhe's psychic involvement created much unnecessary drama.

"I would not do that if I were you," said Levendria from the woods when Rydan set out to demolish the fruit.

Rydan stepped away from the plant, terrified that it had obtained a consciousness. The Sidhe quietly emerged from the tree line and approached Rydan, who appeared less terrified than he should have been. I guess with living in constant fear of the Brothers, Rydan was used to unusual creatures materializing unexpectedly. Realizing their appearance and demeanor were nothing like that of his former enemies, Rydan relaxed. "Why do you care what happens to this plant?"

"That plant might very well be what saves this world and those beyond," stated Analira.

"I find that hard to believe," said Rydan doubtfully.

"I would expect someone with your special talents to be more open-minded," said Vaeris.

Rydan looked around to be sure Saraleast wasn't in hearing range then replied, "All right, you have my attention."

"There are worlds, ours included, that thrive off of a magical Balance. But it hangs on the verge of extinction. Without it, we are doomed," explained Levendria.

"Does this depressing story come with a happy ending?" he asked sarcastically, secretly concerned.

"It does. You see, on a nearby planet lives a woman who wields great power—the power to restore the Balance. But she cannot complete this mission alone. She requires the assistance of someone from your lineage. That individual has yet to arrive, and it is our belief that your creation here can bring forth that person," said Levendria.

"Let me see if I understand. You want another person to eat this fruit, and, what? Fall in love with my daughter, and begin a supernatural lineage? Do you realize how insane that sounds?" he asked incredulously.

The Sidhe exchanged nervous glances and Vaeris replied, "We understand your hesitation, but it has been prophesied."

"All right. Say my daughter *does* begin a line of supernatural beings. If I don't destroy this fruit, what's stopping all of Galaseya from coming across it?" Rydan challenged.

"Us. Like the Brothers on Darmentraea, we are part of Galaseya. We will deter anyone we deem unworthy of your daughter away from the fruit," said Analira.

"Do I have a say in this?" asked Rydan.

"I'm sorry, but destiny does not allow room for one to decide," said Levendria, before the trio disappeared.

I was livid with the Sidhes' performance. They'd blatantly lied to Rydan and even took credit for the visions I'd told them about! But, there was nothing Emrys or I could do to stop them. These were powerful creatures intent on saving their world. I couldn't fault them for that, as I was doing the same. But their methods of fulfilling my visions were less than ethical.

When Saraleast grew older, she discovered she could turn herself into a spirit form and travel between worlds.

This proved useful for years to come. Rydan began experimenting to learn of what elements her abilities consisted of, to see if there were any similarities to his or even future generations. Fortunately, they were able to investigate freely, as not many Galaseyans dared to venture far from the village. Those who did never made it as far as Rydan's house. When Saraleast began testing the boundaries of her own powers even more, she discovered that unlike her father, she had limitations.

Rydan became so enthralled with his research that he almost didn't hear his now eighteen-year-old Saraleast call for him.

"Father! Please come quickly!" exclaimed Saraleast.

Rydan raced through the house to find his daughter searching for him upstairs. He reached the second-floor landing and saw her fearful expression.

"What? Are you hurt?" he asked, examining her for injuries.

"I'm fine, Father, but I fear someone else is not! I overheard the Brothers concocting a disastrous plan to remove another innocent person from Darmentraea," Saraleast cried.

"But why . . ." Rydan started. He was interrupted by an unusual sight out of a nearby window. The sky opened up and spewed out a small figure near an area riddled with various rock formations. Rydan knew that even a strong, full-grown adult couldn't survive a fall like that.

"I'm sorry, my dear. That person is beyond our help," Rydan said somberly.

But the Sidhe took great interest in the new arrival. They buffered his fall and guided the weary, hungry traveler toward Rydan and Saraleast. Now, there are five known villages in Galaseya, and I believe after the Protectors came, other villages were expanding to the outer regions. But each village had a specialty. The port village where Amber's family eventually resided consisted of mostly fishing. Farther inland there are villages specializing in mining, textiles, farming, all sorts of things. And trade became common among the different groups, although they didn't occur as frequently as the years went on. The only commonality between these groups of people was their hospitality, and many of them offered to help the new arrival, but their kindness scared him away. Their behavior was not something he was accustomed to. Within days, he found his way back to outside Rydan's home.

The boy had nearly finished devouring the fruit by the time Saraleast and her father found him. Although Saraleast looked puzzled by his wardrobe, Rydan immediately knew that he came from Darmentraea and was the one they'd seen falling from the sky just days before. Rydan felt compassion for him.

"What's your name?" asked the older man kindly.

The boy glanced between Rydan and Saraleast, not knowing how to react to the gentle words.

"Dugon," he finally replied in a quiet voice. "My name is Dugon Grunewald."

And from then on, Dugon became part of the family. He and Saraleast approached their young adult years as brother and sister, although the Sidhe wanted them to start the powerful lineage. I found a little humor in their failed attempts to control everything. But that didn't stop them from trying. Dugon and Saraleast ended up practicing their powers under the watchful eye of Rydan, who took careful notes. Soon, magic practice became boring which resulted in the pair venturing off to explore the nearest village. This is where they fell in love with a couple of villagers. It was so nice to know that some type of normalcy found its way into their lives. But that feeling quickly dissipated when the Sidhe paid Rydan another visit.

"You have followed our orders exceptionally well," said Levendria, pleased.

"Well, I'm glad you approve," he said, rolling his eyes.

Analira attempted to calm his consternation. "Your part is nearly finished. We ask only that you have your daughter give the fruit to her lover."

"I understand your desire to have an all-powerful lineage. But what if Mattreylar refuses? Will you force the spouses of all my descendants to eat the fruit as well?" Rydan questioned them.

"That is not your concern," Levendria warned.

Regretting helping them in their quest to restore the Balance, Rydan sighed and shook his head. "You're right: this whole Balance and 'worlds in danger' situation isn't really my problem. I only *offered* my help. But, let me tell you something about humans. You can watch us all you'd like and for that matter, try to guide us down the path you want. But at the end of the day, humans will do what they want, and there's nothing you can do to control them."

"We shall see," Levendria said, her eyes narrowing.

From that point on, Rydan never trusted the Sidhe again. And he had a valid point; humans were unpredictable, something the Sidhe would find out the hard way. Rydan revealed to Saraleast and Dugon the truth of the Sidhe and his conspiring with them. But he withheld the information that the beings wanted to control all humans. He did this intentionally, just to challenge the Sidhe. And although Emrys and I didn't condone that behavior, we found it amusing.

Dugon's wife ended up taking the fruit too; she later had the ability to deflect anyone's ability back onto themselves. It was quite unique, but also terrifying. The Sidhe were furious that Dugon planned this, to say the least. They wanted everything done their way. But at this point, they were now in no position to stop the couple from eating the fruit, as it'd just continue to make matters worse. It is said that the Sidhe wanted to "free Rydan from the burden of destroying the plant," but that's not entirely what happened. They threw a tantrum, in a sense. They thought humans were easily understood and believed their plan to be infallible. But the truth was, they didn't like being proven wrong and to an extent thought they were perfect. Something they would find to be false for years to come. Again, they decided to take matters into their own hands and that's why they burned the plant.

Did it free Rydan? Sure it did. But even the benign Sidhe had a dark side.

But this small deviation created a chaos no one was prepared for—not even me. Saraleast and Dugon had their own ideas for restoring the Balance. Saraleast believed it was her duty to oversee everything with her ghost-like powers, and Dugon fervently believed his line alone would produce the Protector that the Sidhe spoke of. This created unimaginable turmoil between the two families, generating a rift between the pair who had once been as close as brother and sister. It's my belief that this is where the centuries of problems began. Two families with the same goal, but different paths to it. As it turned out, Dugon had the right idea, yet he was still way off. But he wouldn't know for hundreds of years.

The estranged surrogate siblings had one child each. Saraleast had Claemar, and Dugon had Marsacor. Claemar's life was exceptionally ordinary, at least within his family lineage. His father, Mattreylar, could no longer tolerate the life of a near immortal, supernatural being. He left his wife and twelve-year-old son to fend for themselves. And they did pretty well, all things considered. In fact, when Saraleast was off saving the Balance, little Claemar found comfort in his best friend, Marsacor. I know—it came as a surprise to all of us as well.

There could not have been a more opposite friendship. Marsacor had been through years of psychic and emotional abuse, starting from infancy. His mother didn't know how to control her power. This might seem like a harmless situation, but it became chaotic during Marsacor's rebellious teenage years. The Sidhe told me of a tragic event that occurred when Marsacor became of magical age. He and his mother were in a heated conversation and he attempted to use his newly discovered illusionary power to stop the arguing, but his mother, Janeralyra, counteracted the attempt. This strike not only confused the young man, but permanently altered his perception of the world. His green eyes turned a crazed, muddy green, matching his new personality.

Marsacor fell unconscious from the initial attack. Angered and afraid for his son, Dugon retaliated and confronted his wife, who was prepared to use her gift on him. Dugon tapped into his old Darmentraean ways and used his powers of suppression on Janeralyra as she was about to attack. The result was deadly. The combined powers caused her mind to implode.

From that point on, Dugon felt he could trust no one else. He created extreme rules in his home, emphasizing to the impressionable Marsacor that romance didn't exist and he should only choose a companion for procreation purposes. I won't even begin to say what choice words he used when describing the Oaks. Yes, the descendants of my cousin John. Somehow, these specific people always came up in his rants about how they'd made life so miserable for him. Due to the new addition to his gifts, Marsacor saw through much of these claims and secretly had no opinions about the Oaks.

The day Claemar and Marsacor met was not only unique, but ironically poetic. Both traveled to the port village in search of food and supplies. They had seen each other before, but Marsacor's rough demeanor made Claemar rather nervous. But Claemar found himself in a predicament with a merchant who refused to trade with the young, happy man. Marsacor leaned against a nearby cart, casually eating fruit. He'd been hoping to establish himself in the village as a force to be reckoned with, and as Claemar floundered in his bartering attempts, Marsacor saw the perfect moment to interrupt.

"So sorry, I couldn't help but overhear. It seems my friend here is offering you a trade you desperately need," said Marsacor, looking down at a box of what appeared to be soap. The merchant scowled at Marsacor as Claemar stared at him, mouth open in shock.

"Is that so?" growled the dealer.

"Yes, and if I were you, I'd take the offer before you drive every woman away with your stench," Marsacor snapped, his crazed eyes glaring at the nervous merchant.

Grumbling, the trader threw a bundle of clothes toward Marsacor's opened arms and snatched the box of soap from Claemar. The young man stared incredulously at the strange man who handed him the clothes with a brusque, "You're welcome."

"I didn't require your assistance!" exclaimed Claemar, coming out of his stupor.

Marsacor continued walking away, his smirk hidden. "Clearly you did, or that so-called trade would've been a complete disaster."

"I've handled far worse merchants than him," Claemar objected.

Marsacor spun around and shrugged. "I couldn't tell by your performance."

"What have I ever done to you?" asked Claemar.

A quizzical look crossed Marsacor's face. He shook his head and said, "Nothing."

"Then why are you cross with me?" Claemar prodded.

Feeling increasingly uncomfortable, Marsacor replied, "I . . . I'm not cross; that's just how I am."

"That type of behavior will never attract a friend."

Marsacor scoffed. "I never said I was looking for a friend."

Now just a few inches apart, Claemar nodded and smiled, his caring heart seeing straight through Marsacor's coarse facade. "Yes, you did. When you came to assist me with a merchant that I have dealt with many times before."

9

I can't say the rest is history, because Claemar and Marsacor's friendship should never be overlooked. These two men, from opposite walks of life, defied all of the odds and formed a friendship that, despite future events, remains eternal. Marsacor brought out the edge in Claemar, and Claemar showed Marsacor that he had a loving heart under all the masks that he forced the world to see. As far as I know, Claemar was the only member of the Oak family, aside from the twins, that Marsacor really liked. Something about the Oaks having a self-righteous attitude, which I can understand, but his family had problems too—something I'm sure he spent years trying to forget.

I don't think even the Sidhe could've picked a better camaraderie. These two men eventually came across a situation that would prove once and for all that their friendship was genuine. It must've been at least two years after they met that they found themselves deep in the Galaseyan woods. They discovered a deep cave they figured was worth exploring for hidden treasure. But this cave was riddled with so many other caverns and tunnels that the boys lost their way, and their lanterns ran out of fuel. As their last source of light extinguished, Claemar's body began to glow bright and shining, illuminating the entire tunnel. Throughout his life, Claemar had had no desire to practice his gift, much to his mother's aggravation. But this created a problem, as his gift now only revealed itself when he was afraid.

Claemar hung his head as his friend stared in awe.

"I know. You must hate me," Claemar said after minutes of silence.

It was obvious to Marsacor that Claemar was of the dreaded Oak family his father had warned him about. But it made no sense to him. There was nothing evil about

Claemar. At that moment, Marsacor decided to do something that would change his life forever.

"I can't hate you, Claemar. If I did, I'd only be hating myself," Marsacor replied kindly.

Following Claemar's confused, nervous glance, Marsacor proceeded to plant vivid images in his mind of the Galaseyan animals. Claemar's expression turned to that of horror as he replied, "You are a Grunewald. But how? I was told your family was ruthless and cruel."

"They might be that way, but I'm not! At least, not anymore, thanks to you," said Marsacor adamantly.

"How?" asked Claemar skeptically.

"You taught me that it's better to show compassion," Marsacor replied.

Claemar still showed signs of hesitation, so Marsacor continued: "Look at us, Claemar! We come from opposing clans. We prove their actions don't define us as individuals. Maybe one day we may even unite our families, and join forces to fight? Be heroes!"

"That is a fairy tale, Marsacor," said Claemar, shrugging it off.

"Is it? According to the rest of the world, our *powers* are fairy tales." Marsacor held out a hand. "Join me, brother, and let's be heroes!"

For a while we all thought these two were of the people I had seen in my visions, but sadly, dark forces were at work, and their dreams of being heroes faded. Quite literally, I might add. Marsacor and Claemar both found love and continued their family lines. But that didn't stop them from spending time together. It just gave them more obligations to tend to and stories to share with each other. But as time went on, Marsacor felt his relationship with Claemar strained, though it had nothing to do with any disagreements.

Strange images flooded Marsacor's mind, images that seemed to foretell terrible events that spoke of his friend's doom. He began questioning his own sanity, wondering if his powers were malfunctioning. Asking Dugon was out of the question, as he was still unaware of the forbidden friendship. And Marsacor knew Rydan from brief moments in his childhood, but not well enough to come to him for this kind of help. The only solution was to bear the disturbing images and hope they'd go away. But ignoring them seemed to aggravate things more. The images soon came with pounding headaches.

Eventually, Marsacor approached Claemar and warned him of future danger. Naturally, Claemar was concerned, but since Marsacor's talent did not reside in visions, Claemar ended up disregarding the warnings. If it weren't for the incessant headaches and realistic images, Marsacor would have, too.

Marsacor's and Claemar's children must have been of magical age when Marsacor lost everything. It was a spring morning and Claemar's wife, Craeya, told Marsacor her husband had ventured off to the caves in search of the treasure they'd sought when the boys were younger. Panic quickly set in, as this was the beginning to Marsacor's visions. He raced to his childhood playground and endlessly searched for his friend, calling his name until his voice was hoarse. He almost believed Claemar returned home until he heard a faint voice calling for him.

At the end of a tunnel, Marsacor saw his friend alive and called, "Claemar, there is no treasure! Why are you here?"

"You told me to meet you—I've been searching for you!" he hollered back.

Something was definitely wrong. At least, Marsacor came to this conclusion rather quickly as he replied, "Let's speak outside. It isn't safe in here anymore."

As Claemar's glowing body started toward Marsacor, a deafening rumble shook the cavern. Marsacor stood frozen in horror as the ceiling came crashing down on his friend, extinguishing his light. All their yelling had created a cave-in. The cavern Marsacor stood in threated to be next. He forced his lead-like legs to move toward the exit. The unsteady structure soon caught up with him and he was forced to crawl out on his stomach.

When the rubble subsided and his lungs were free of the dust, Marsacor lifted his aching body to see that it was true: his friend was gone forever. And someone was behind it.

"That went better than I thought—great plan, Brother," came a cold voice.

Marsacor jumped to his feet, ready to indulge his anger. But, he came face-to-face with the Brothers, who looked all too pleased to see his reaction.

"Who are you?" asked Marsacor.

"I'd say your worst nightmare, but I'm pretty sure that back there is," said Petraylin, pointing to the wreckage behind Marsacor.

Marsacor glared at the Brothers. "*You* planted those images in my mind and tricked Claemar. Why?"

"We are the Masters of Illusion, Marsacor. We do as we please," said Martheykos. "Besides, we merely wanted to show you that life can't be perfect, even on Galaseya. You're welcome!"

Memories from his childhood raced through Marsacor's mind. These were the Brothers in one of many of Rydan's stories. And from what Marsacor knew of these rulers, the Brothers always had an ulterior motive. This wasn't a typical visit, and Marsacor was determined to deter them from their true purpose.

"I'll stop you," he said determinedly. "Whatever it is you're planning for me or this world, it won't work."

Petraylin chuckled as Martheykos approached his challenger. Their eyes met as the villain stopped mere inches from his new victim.

"I don't know what Rydan told you about us, but we don't need to have an underlying plan to wreak havoc on you humans," Martheykos hissed, his wicked black eyes burning a hole in Marsacor's weak soul.

For a moment their eyes were deadlocked, until Martheykos turned away. He began walking away from Marsacor when he paused. He turned as a grin distorted his pale, smooth face. "If I ever have a plan, Marsacor, I promise, you'll be the first to know!"

I wasn't even technically there, and those words still haunt me hundreds of years later. The Brothers didn't know what the Sidhe were planning about restoring the Balance. But they grew suspicious in that moment, and it wasn't Marsacor's fault. He was simply another toy to play with . . .

a toy that fought back. His unfortunate reaction is what led to a series of tragedies and struggles in both families. But each time the Brothers left their planet to cause mischief, Saraleast used that opportunity to infiltrate their world and form a group, now known as the Elders.

It wasn't always that easy, though. She got this idea from Crais, Dugon's brother. When he died, leaving his son alone in the underground cavern, she decided this was a sign that the Grunewalds of Darmentraea needed to ban together, in the hope that they would one day take back their world as it once was—a less dark version of what it had become. When Danin, Crais's son, grew up, Saraleast approached him with this idea, and that's how the Elders were truly formed. Now, this was challenging, as many of the future generations of Grunewalds wanted to live out their life in relative freedom. But once the Brothers started using the majority of them as target practice, possibly just to keep them in line, the family realized they would be better off living in hiding and only come out when truly necessary. Believe me, keeping a wild family like that in line was hard, even for a powerful woman like Saraleast, but she did it. And this became our only aspect of hope in the dark times that lay ahead.

Marsacor was never the same again after Claemar's untimely death. He slipped back into his dark ways. This was some point after his son's birth, possibly a year or less. All I know is Marsacor's wife expressed her gratefulness over Claemar's death, as she rarely saw her husband when his friend was alive. That didn't go over well. In a fit of rage, Marsacor killed her. But the unofficial story was that he grew tired of her. I assume this was to hide the truth of his friendship from his family.

His downward spiral eased when his son, Davylar, now fully grown, fell in love with Stephria, Claemar's daughter. He often saw Davylar sneak away from the house, and he felt a twinge of pride. This wasn't to say he completely approved of Stephria. To Marsacor she seemed almost too perfect and good, but she was Claemar's daughter and Marsacor knew he'd want to unite the families and stop the constant feuding. There was some good in this dark family. But unlike his father, Davylar's talent didn't lie in the art of deception. Dugon quickly discovered his grandson was not following his rules of romance.

Naturally, Dugon instructed Marsacor to "take care" of the situation however he saw fit. I felt sorry for him! Stopping those two lovers was almost an insult to Claemar's memory. Marsacor constantly warred with himself, feeling conflicted about his father's commands. I ended up presenting an idea to the Sidhe, Emrys, and Saraleast, who had recently joined forces with us. The idea? Tell Marsacor the truth about everything. The Brothers had become our enemies, and Marsacor probably hated them more than anyone, so I figured he'd be better with us than against us.

My proposal was well accepted among our group. In fact, Saraleast offered to approach Marsacor, and it was instantly unanimous. She was the only one of us who could not only provide comfort—after all, she was Claemar's mother—but also hope, a feeling Marsacor was in need of. I remember their conversation: powerful and surprising. It took place one evening when Marsacor was about to confront Davylar about Stephria. He stood at the edge of the forest, staring up into a window of his family home, Davylar framed there in plain view.

"Marsacor, wait!" Saraleast's voice rang through the trees.

Marsacor spun around, expecting to see the Brothers playing a trick. But when Saraleast materialized in front of him, he remembered the stories of Rydan's daughter.

"Saraleast, right?" he asked, hoping it was she.

She smiled and nodded, and just like that, the introductions were out of the way. But her tone became serious when she said, "I know what you're about to do, but I only ask that you please listen to what I have to say first."

Marsacor looked around for any unwelcome eavesdroppers. Then he turned to Saraleast and gave her a curt nod. "Go on."

"I have journeyed between the worlds, and the Brothers have grown wary of your family," she said. There was no way for her to know what his father had told him.

"I'm not sure why. Their fight is with me," he replied, walking away from his house.

"That is not entirely true. Their quarrel is with anyone they wish," Saraleast replied simply.

In the dim light of the night, Marsacor's eyebrows furrowed as he said, "Saraleast, what aren't you telling me?"

She heaved a sigh. "I'm part of an elite group of individuals whose sole purpose in life is to restore the Balance that this world and others thrive on. If we are unfortunate enough to have the Brothers discover our plan, they'll stop at nothing to see it destroyed."

"Okay," Marsacor replied, still confused. "And what does this have to do with me and my family?"

"Everything," Saraleast said with a kind smile. "Neither I nor my friends can restore the Balance alone. It has been foretold that someone in your family is destined to save us all."

"Any idea who that might be?" asked Marsacor, playing along.

"No—unfortunately, all I was told is that it will be three people, born of our magic," she replied, her tone guilty.

"That could also describe the Oak family," Marsacor said with a smirk.

Saraleast shook her head, perhaps frustrated that the conversation wasn't going as planned. "I am aware. That's why I've come to you for help."

"My help? What could I possibly do?" Marsacor laughed.

"You can create a diversion. Make the Brothers believe that you want nothing to do with them, and that your family and the Oaks know nothing of them or the Balance. Become invisible," she replied.

Marsacor walked back toward the tree line and looked up into the same window as before. Davylar had gone to bed, as had Dugon. As much as he admired Saraleast and her friends for wanting to save the world, he couldn't help.

"I'm sorry, but I can't. Any diversion would require me to create unnecessary chaos in my family, and I can't do that. They've been through enough as it is—both families have."

"Your devotion to my son is quite admirable, even after his death. I saw how his friendship changed you. But ask yourself this: If he were having this discussion with us, what do you think he'd do?"

"He would never ask me to destroy my family over a concept, let alone one that I'm receiving very little information on," he snapped.

"Marsacor, I never asked you to destroy your family. I'm asking for a mere diversion. However you decide to create it is your decision alone—as are the consequences," she replied tensely.

Marsacor stared at her in shock. "How does this make you any different from the Brothers?"

Anger filled her eyes. Being compared to the Brothers, even by today's standards, is worse than being cursed. But despite her rage, she gave a pretty valid answer.

"I have a purpose in my mission, and that is to save mankind from extinction, not to toy with it," Saraleast said as she began to turn into a spectral form to make her exit. "What is *your* purpose, Marsacor?"

After that conversation, Marsacor and Saraleast didn't have the best of relationships. But her words gave him something to think about. Now, I wouldn't say he found his purpose, but he did make a decision, one that left a permanent scar. He began enacting his plan by spying on the Oak family. He studied their habits and conveniently placed himself in the port village where they spent much of their time. And what he discovered about this family made him alter his original plan several times.

Stephria's mother speculated that her daughter was seeing someone in secret. And like a Galaseyan, she never confronted her daughter. She merely assumed that since Stephria was keeping the relationship hidden, there might have been something shady about the man's character. Stephria's mother pressed upon her to find another man. But Stephria took after her father and wanted to follow her heart.

Hoping his idea would be simple, Marsacor led an attractive and kind man to Stephria, influencing them to fall in love with his illusions. Stephria did marry this man, just to appease her aging mother, but she continued to see Davylar in secret. Since Davylar hardly ever went into the village, he never knew she was married. And Stephria was very good at sneaking out of the house when her husband was off working. It was the perfect plan; neither man ever knew of the other.

Marsacor figured his job was done, and his son and Stephria would separate by themselves, but Stephria was good at keeping secrets. So good, in fact, that neither of the men knew she was pregnant with Davylar's child. Stephria finally confessed everything to her mother, who didn't necessarily approve of her daughter's affair, but didn't condemn her for it either. Marsacor found out rather quickly, as it didn't take him long to detect a strange energy field around Stephria, just a small part of his gift. He had the ability to see if an Oak or Grunewald were carrying children. I think this ability extends to any child of magic, but I'm not entirely sure. To hide the illegitimate child, he used his gifts on Stephria, manipulating her into giving her child up for adoption. He would then come in and take the child, raising it in secret with his family.

He'd had no issues secretly involving himself in Stephria's life, making her fall in love with someone else. And now that Davylar's child was on its way, there was no telling when the father-to-be would discover everything. During Stephria's pregnancy, Marsacor kept a close eye on Davylar, making sure for those nine months that they didn't meet. Everything worked out for the best, but when the new addition to the Grunewald family arrive, it became harder to hide the secret. Marsacor had a plan for destroying the family, but a child wasn't it. Well, fast-forward three years, and Stephria is still bouncing between both men, while her new son, Jermiar, remains at home, out of his mother's drama. But his intelligence was twice what would be expected for his age, even at three years old. He suspected his mother was hiding something.

With Jermiar safely out of the way, Marsacor continued with his plan. This time, he used his illusions to nudge Davylar in a specific direction, and from there Davylar's paranoia drove him the rest of the way. He discovered

Stephria's infidelity and tried to reason with her. She claimed she had no feelings for her husband and that it was all for appearances. Which was actually the truth, although the Oaks stayed out of society to hide their unusual aging, they maintained a respectable role in Galaseyan society. Davylar accepted her word as truth for the time being, and that caused Marsacor to formulate yet another plan.

But he never got the chance. Apparently, the Brothers became intrigued by the drama and decided to *lend a hand*. This was an unexpected element as the family wasn't affecting the Brother's plans. At the rate things were going, anything Marsacor decided on would inevitably result in the Brothers getting involved. We all agreed it was better for them to aid in the destruction of a family than the destruction of the human race. Pick your battles, right?

In their own conniving way, they urged Davylar to see Stephria one evening when she and her husband were out for an evening stroll. I don't know what Davylar overheard, exactly, but he was under the false impression that Stephria was professing her love to her husband. And it set him over the edge. Davylar followed them home that night; Marsacor trailed behind his son from a safe distance. He watched as Davylar entered the house, then sneaked in behind his son. Marsacor knew nothing positive would come of this and the only thing he could do was protect Jermiar—his grandson.

Unfortunately, all attempts of shielding the child from the impending doom were quickly dashed as Davylar's footsteps sounded on the stairs, causing Jermiar to wake. As he poked his head out from his doorway, Marsacor quickly ducked into a nearby room, his heart racing. Jermiar's little feet pitter-pattered up the stairs toward his parents' room.

Marsacor silently followed behind, slipping into nearby rooms and shadows when he needed to. Both Marsacor and Jermiar stopped at a partially opened door. Marsacor was well hidden. The dim candlelight from the room shone on the boy's terrified face. Stephria mumbled something unintelligible, but Marsacor heard a reply that made him cringe.

"No more lies!" cried Davylar.

Streaks of lightning lit up the room, not only killing Stephria's husband, but a stray spark jumping toward the doorway and accidentally striking Jermiar in the mouth. The boy almost fell down the stairs from the force. Disregarding his own safety, Marsacor caught Jermiar and sat him on the stairs just as Davylar sped down.

Little Jermiar never forgot what Marsacor did . . . which proved to be a problem several days later when Jermiar and Stephria confronted the Grunewald family at their home. Dugon, Marsacor, and Davylar came outside to see Stephria's tear-stained face and young Jermiar's tiny fists clenched in as much rage a young child could muster.

This very situation came as no surprise to Dugon who was waiting for some catastrophe to strike. When Davylar came home the night of the murder looking frantic, Dugon had calmed him down and gotten the whole story of the night's events out of his grandson. Dugon didn't seem to mind, and Marsacor acted like nothing was wrong, but truthfully, he had no idea how to fix this.

"How could you, Davylar?" was all Stephria could utter.

"Don't play innocent with me: I heard you professing your love to your husband," Davylar spat.

"I was not!" Stephria gasped in horror. "I confessed to him about our relationship! I was prepared to leave him for you!"

"If you had told me, none of this would have happened!" he exclaimed.

"I . . . I was uncertain myself until the very moment I told him about us," she replied quietly.

"You mean it was so hard to choose between us? I thought you loved me!" Davylar nearly growled, the tips of his fingers glowing, threatening to spark.

Seeing this conversation was going south rather quickly, Marsacor jumped between the feuding families and held up his hands in surrender. "Whoa! Okay, I see my plan took a bit of a different turn than I expected," he lied, secretly hoping the Brothers would hear this challenging remark.

"Marsacor?" asked Dugon curiously.

His next move even took me by surprise. The illusion of all illusions. Through his voice, he used his power to manipulate everyone. To this day, I don't know how he managed to do it, as all magic has its limitations, aside from Rydan's. But, I have a sneaking suspicion he made a double deal with Emrys through the Sidhe. Only Emrys with his infinite knowledge of the magical Balance plane could offer the assistance Marsacor needed in this moment.

"This was all my doing. I planted the ideas of love and murder in Stephria's and Davylar's heads," he replied.

"Why would you do such a thing, Father?" Davylar questioned, horrified.

"Mostly because I was bored," he replied nonchalantly. "And anyway, no real loss—you're too good for her kind."

"My . . . kind?" she echoed, insulted by this stranger. "What do you mean by that?"

"I mean," Marsacor replied, inching threateningly toward her, "that if you don't leave our home this moment, your child will discover what life's like as an orphan."

Marsacor hated playing the bad guy, but due to all the secrecy and the sake of . . . well the future, he had to be. Even when Davylar discovered that the youngest Grunewald was actually his, he couldn't look at the child the same way again. Marsacor took it upon himself to take care of the child who he named, Huntinylar. In many ways, I find Marsacor the most heroic of them all. Even when Amber arrived, he made it a point to act as if he were oblivious, just like the rest. I think in some ways he tried to drop subtle hints to Amber that he knew more than he let on; it was his only way of redeeming himself in a sense. That's why he took on the task of bringing her back into the family.

But there are some members of the Oak family that still couldn't forgive him for the words he said. He was so convincing when he cast the blame on himself that Stephria saw true fierceness in Marsacor's eyes. She grabbed Jermiar's small hand and dragged him away from the scene. The little boy looked behind him, starring at Marsacor. He knew this man had saved him, and he'd spend one hundred years trying to find out why.

The only information Jermiar could get out of his mom was that the Grunewalds had power too, but were dark. Jermiar spent most of his days gathering information from locals who heard of rumors of magic, but everything he obtained was speculative, including local superstition about Sidhe sightings. He collected so much information that he ended up building a library off of his family home. But with of all the knowledge he gained, he still had no idea why Marsacor spared his life if indeed the man had planned his father's murder.

This small fact bothered Jermiar for so long that he eventually decided to confront Marsacor, despite his mother's warnings. But he never made it to the Grunewald house. It would seem that fate had a better idea. Far deep in the woods on the way to his destination, Jermiar heard a conversation, one he was certain was not meant for his ears.

"Look, all I'm saying is I think Petraylin and I could use a mind like yours. After all, you *are* part Darmentraean," insisted Martheykos.

"Yes, but I'm also Galaseyan. And weren't you the ones who kicked my father off your planet? He's darker than I am!" said Marsacor.

Petraylin chuckled. "Sure, but he's not the one who broke his son's heart just because he was bored. I wouldn't dismiss that darkness inside of you. You have great potential, Marsacor."

Jermiar stared at Marsacor through the trees as a ghost of a smile appeared on his face. His suspicions were correct after all these years. Marsacor had a hidden motive, and Jermiar had to find out what that was.

"You're right. But, I'm not dark or naïve enough to be manipulated by your charismatic charm," he replied sarcastically.

Martheykos looked at Petraylin as a wicked grin flashed across his face. "I don't know, Petraylin. I think this dilemma is something we can fix."

Simultaneously, the Brothers menacingly raised their hands toward Marsacor, who tried counteracting whatever illusion they threw his way. But it was an unfair fight, and Jermiar saw this coming. Without thinking twice, Jermiar jumped from his woodland hiding spot and lunged to Marsacor's side, placing a firm grip on his shoulder.

Marsacor wasn't sure what to think when he felt a sudden burst of power, but he wasn't expecting to see Jermiar out of the corner of his eye. Now that the Brothers met their match—or, rather, couldn't easily overtake Marsacor—they fled the scene.

Before I go into the next part of the story, I'd like to clear up one major question: Where were the Sidhe? Well, Emrys and I had a heart-to-heart talk with them about consistently interfering with human lives. After all the disastrous mistakes they made, we finally got through to them that people needed to make their own decisions. And let me just say that scolding otherworldly beings is quite strange.

When the Brothers left and Jermiar and Marsacor were alone in the woods, silence took up the beginning of their conversation.

"There, now we're even." Jermiar mumbled., "Now I would like some answers."

Marsacor cringed; he knew this conversation might come up eventually, but like the rest of us, he'd hoped it would be later. He leaned against a nearby tree, trying to catch his breath from the exhausting ordeal, when he said, "What do you want to know?"

"You spared my life all those years ago. Why?" Jermiar asked, trying not to sound accusatory.

Marsacor had every reason to be apprehensive at this point. None of us wanted him to reveal too much information as it might leak to the Brothers, but fortunately, he gave Jermiar the bare minimum. He went on to explain that the destruction of both families was necessary to protect the greater good. Marsacor did his best to convince Jermiar that he didn't care one way or another about him or his mother. He had to lie a little, though Jermiar saw through that. But his inquisitive mind heard the urgency in Marsacor's tone to keep this a secret. Jermiar walked away from that conversation with less hatred toward the Grunewalds and more irritation . . . at least for now.

10

As history shows, Jermiar eventually got caught up in the loop with Marsacor, and soon the two men put their differences and past aside to fight toward a common goal. I believe even when Amber came around, the two still maintained a secret camaraderie. But the Sidhes' interference in their lives didn't make that easy. Just like with Marsacor, they believed Jermiar could be a strong asset. These two men were of the last of the "inner circle" in our battle for the Balance. But they knew nothing of my true past or identity. I have to admit, though, I really respected them for keeping up appearances and not giving too much away to Amber or the rest of the family. Regardless of how much we tried to keep relative peace until the vision came true, it didn't always work. Especially when Jermiar met Huntinylar, his half-brother.

To say they loathed each other was a great understatement. Of course, it wasn't always that way. Initially they had no opinions of each other, but then, *she* came. Maelia. The light of both their eyes. In my opinion, this woman belonged on Darmentraea. She toyed with those brothers' minds, and unlike Stephria, Maelia reveled in the attention. Little did she know just how deadly her game would become. Maelia eventually ended up with Huntinylar and they had two daughters, but that didn't stop Jermiar's bitterness. He swore up and down that Huntinylar stole Maelia from him. And it was this thought that made him do something a Darmentraean would be proud of.

Even after the girls were born, Maelia occasionally journeyed to the village for supplies, but mostly socialized. It was one of these times that Jermiar confronted her about who her husband really was. Although she seemed nervous about Jermiar's claims that Huntinylar had volatile tendencies, she disregarded the fact that her husband had powers.

So Jermiar had to take drastic measures. He knew that Huntinylar had explosive anger issues and even the slightest disagreement could set him off. And what better way to prove this to Maelia than to make a public example of Huntinylar?

"Will you please leave us alone?" asked Huntinylar. "Can we not simply let this feud rest?"

"No, I will not let this rest! Maelia deserves to know what sort of family she married into!" Jermiar protested.

Offended, Huntinylar stared at Jermiar. "Brother, you know no one chose their powers. We were born into it, just like you!"

"Oh! *Both* of you wield powers! How fascinating!" Maelia said, smiling. What she really meant was, *Oh, who's stronger, and how can I use you?*

"Fascinating is not the word I would use. Deadly, perhaps," Jermiar spat.

"My power might be harmful, but I've never used it against any human or creature!" Huntinylar insisted, giving in to Jermiar's taunting.

"Yet! What's preventing you from accidentally harming Maelia?" Jermiar challenged, seeing small wisps of clouds emerging from Huntinylar's fingertips.

"Unlike you, I love Maelia. All you seem interested in is stealing her from me!" Huntinylar exclaimed, his power crawling up his arms.

"Love? Your family is incapable of such emotion. Just ask your murderous father," Jermiar hissed, knowing the truth of Davylar's deeds.

And just as Jermiar had planned, Huntinylar directed his acidic power toward his half brother. The devious man jumped out of striking range and grabbed Huntinylar's wrist. Unfortunately, a small wisp grazed Maelia's cheek. It was a minor burn, but the incident left such an emotional impression on her that she drifted away from both families.

Huntinylar and Jermiar never let their feud rest. Yes, it was Jermiar's fault initially, but he fully believed he was in the right, which just made the situation worse.

While the two families continued with their ridiculous feud, Rydan jumped on the Balance bandwagon. For years, he' had the idea that the more people who knew of the weak Balance, the better. He wanted an army. We tried to make him see reason, but he'd already managed to wrap the people around his finger. He began the idea of a monarchy and, over time, inserted himself in the group as a court physician, but it didn't last too long. Soon, his claims of the Balance, started sounding conspiratorial more than anything.

Although the monarchy did nothing to our cause, it provided a good distraction to the people while Huntinylar's daughters grew up. Joyra, the eldest, made quite a name for herself when she found love. Everyone in the family warned her against Nyelar. He was known among the villagers as a ladies' man. He was very sneaky around Joyra—he knew she came from a powerful family of sorts, and to him, power meant stature.

Joyra refused to cater to the rumors about the man of her dreams . . . until she discovered the painful truth herself. She spotted him fondling a pretty young woman behind a building in the village. Instead of being a rational human being and end the relationship, Joyra, with her flair for the dramatic, took it a step further. She waited until he was alone, working in his garden as most Galaseyans did.

"Joyra! My love! You are looking as beautiful as ever!" Nyelar expressed, his tone as fake as his smile.

"Is that what you say to all your lady friends?" she snapped.

Nyelar put down his spade and innocently replied, "My love is only for you!"

Joyra stood her ground. "I would like to believe that. But I fear the women of the village would disagree. I am not a fool, Nyelar."

His charismatic smile faded away, and his true arrogant behavior appeared. "Of course you're a fool. I'm certain by now that your family warned you about my . . . character.

Yet you deliberately ignored their claims, thinking you knew me better than they. The only thing differing you from those silly girls of the villages is that you were blind enough to think I cared. There's nothing special about you."

Joyra completely snapped. Her self-esteem was low to begin with, but for someone she once thought loved her to say such harsh words broke something inside her. She stared into his cold eyes and flashed the cutest smile she could muster. She placed a hand on his arm, knowing her power would kick in. His arm began to feel numb as she menacingly said, "You really think you're the only one who concealed the truth?"

Nyelar's body fell completely numb to Joyra's comatose power. The only sense she left him with was his hearing. She buried him there in his garden. As he lay in the deep hole, she casually leaned against a shovel and said, "How poetic, buried in all your lies."

Joyra spent centuries convincing everyone—and herself—that she'd grown bored with Nyelar. Truthfully, the man was beneath her and I believe she could have found love again. But fear crept in and prevented her from trying. She made a silent vow that no one would make her feel weak again. But that didn't exactly stop her from involving herself in the affairs of the heart. It was just the heart of her little sister.

When Holisiana fell in love with Rogalar, Joyra made it her job to cover for her little sister. But when Holisiana was pregnant with Christolar, it became harder to hide the clandestine relationship. Eventually, Dugon discovered her secret and disowned her. She moved in with the Oak family. But Davylar, Huntinylar, and Joyra were excited for her and often met her in secret. Marsacor remained indifferent, only because Rogalar and Holisiana were cousins. But he couldn't say anything or there'd be an all-out battle, and Galaseya wasn't ready for that kind of power explosion. Marsacor's secret would be the least of his worries, as the Sidhe decided to get involved. History says they truly believed Chris was of the predictions, but we all knew that wasn't the case. I just think they got tired of waiting.

When Christolar was born, he was very sick—not because of the Toxin, but because he was the product of incest. I don't know if it would've made a difference if the Sidhe interfered, but I guess it was necessary. Amber severely lacked confidence in who she was, and Christolar provided the extra boost she needed.

And speaking of the twins, we all knew they were coming. Even before Holisiana was pregnant again, Saraleast and Emrys felt a shift in the remaining Balance. Saraleast also found it exhausting to go between worlds. Fearful of her concerns, she confided in me, and only me. Fortunately, Emrys had already come to me prior and said that he felt two children, not just one—benefits of being in the Balance, I suppose. All three of us had a sickening feeling that the Sidhe would try to control the situation when the twins were born. So we had to act fast. Saraleast consulted the Elders, who were now residing underground, and she took particular interest in Kylis. He became her soldier, in a sense. I wouldn't know for many years that she and Emrys knew Ambrose was one of the prophesied.

By the time Holisiana was well into her pregnancy, Stephria used her gift as an ultrasound and announced the double surprise. Because my visions weren't clear, the Sidhe were adamant that while one twin was of great importance, the other had nothing to do with the prophecy. And when they were born, Saraleast had quite a task on her hands. When the Sidhe deliberated sending Ambrose to Darmentraea, Saraleast acted immediately and enlisted the help of a couple from the Elders to take the newborn in. Ambrose was raised separately from the Elders as we all grew concerned that the elite group would pose a threat to the child. The last thing we wanted to do was give the Brothers any reason to think Ambrose would become a threat to them, at least prematurely.

In a way, I'm grateful they sent Ambrose away. At least he wasn't in the middle of his family's drama. But he still dealt with issues regarding life on Darmentraea. Like Kylis, Ambrose promised he would never harm a living person, but that didn't stop him from occasionally stealing. He was never really good at it, considering the multiple beatings he would receive. Ambrose's adoptive parents taught him the best they could without revealing too much about his identity, but they were eventually killed by an unfortunate confrontation with a rogue Darmentraean.

Saraleast spent ten years trying to protect Ambrose after his parents' untimely demise. Considering families were nearly nonexistent, Ambrose's adoptive parents' death seemed like a good thing, only because any suspicious activity, such as a normal family unit, would have alerted the Brothers, who would no doubt intervene. When Ambrose was probably around ten and dying from hunger and the beatings he'd receive from merchants after stealing, Kylis was sent to rescue him and take the boy under his wing. That's when they used the cave as their home.

Prior to this event, Kylis had stolen equipment from the Brothers, whenever they were not lording over their world. The monitors became Saraleast's last effort to save the Balance. None of us were pleased about her sacrifice, but it was a necessary evil. She had all intentions of holding off on her final mission, mostly because I think she believed the Balance would be restored. But when she saved Rydan from Kaleya, it took too much toll on her, and she was forced to enact her plan.

Well, that wraps everything up, as the rest of the story you already know. I guess that leaves one question, though. Why did I delve into the gruesome destruction of Earth? Or, better yet, why did I reveal the scandals of our heroic family? And my response is . . . repeated history. See, I've lived countless lives, and each generation made similar mistakes as the humans on Earth. Now, I'm definitely not targeting my fellow Diraetans. Far from it, actually. Galaseya and especially Darmentraea are at fault for this too. Some repeated mistakes were fixable and minor, but others . . . not so much.

I actually didn't start noticing this pattern until forty years after the Balance was restored. By some miracle, we, the Protectors, finally found where Emrys was physically being held, in a comatose state on Heirsha. With the Balance restored, his prison was now obsolete. Apparently, the healing planet rescued him and had been restoring him all this time—concealing him until his body was fully healed. But he looked nothing like his former self. He now had the qualities of each planet. He had Amber's red veins, Ambrose's blue-black hair, Kylis's green eyes, and my white skin.

The reunion was phenomenal, and the families took to him quite well. But when he saw the industries the Diraetans made and the new technology, he grew concerned that we were heading down another dangerous path—one we might not be able to return from.

With this new age on the rise, Emrys and I believe it is our responsibility as humans to preserve our species, and remember the sacrifices made so that we all might live.

Acknowledgements

Special thanks to my beta readers who saw the potential in this adventurous prequel. I couldn't have done it without your insight and support!

To my fans, thank you so much for encouraging me to continue on! This prequel was for each one of you. I hope that this little side story gives you a better understanding of just some of the planets in the Chronosalis Galaxy!

About the Author

Ceara Comeau started writing stories when she was twelve years old. Her writing career began with "Amber Oak Volume 1" and "Adventures of the Young and Curious". Both books were a compilation of short stories that were self-published when she was fifteen years old. Over the next few years, "Amber Oak Volume 2" was written and became self-published when she was seventeen. During her college years, "Amber Oak and the Missing Links" and "Amber Oak and the Master of Illusions" was born. After they were self-published, Ceara wrote another story separate from her Amber Oak world entitled, "The Lost Journal of Erika Traynor". That was the last book she self-published before graduating college in December 2016. Later, she returned to the beginning and looked at her Amber Oak series. It was then that she decided to take the series she worked hard on all those years ago and rewrite it. It first started out as an eight book novella series, then to a trilogy, and then it turned into one book, "Memories of Chronosalis." Her latest book, "A Scientist's Remorse" is a history of the characters introduced in "Memories of Chronosalis".

www.ingramcontent.com/pod-product-compliance
Lightning Source LLC
Chambersburg PA
CBHW052147170626
46812CB00004B/1623